MY FAE MATE

MISTVALE SPIN-OFF

STELLA RAINBOW

CONTENTS

Dedicated to:
D.S. for helping me make Celeste's story as true to the
community as I could.

ONE

Celeste

"You need to stop working," Mia said as she flew to my side and poked me in the cheek with a perfectly pointed nail.

"Ow! Mia, what the hell?" I demanded as I turned to her, the beads in my braids knocking against each other in a soothing rhythm.

Mia narrowed her eyes at me as she placed her fists on her hips, her lips squished together. Barely three feet in height, the pixie was anything but intimidating, but I knew better than to trust her cute look.

Mia was the leader of my pixies, and she kept them all working in perfect sync. She was the only one of the pixies I maintained steady, direct contact with, and that was more than enough. For being a part of my soul, she was awfully different from me.

"You're always working, Celeste. You need to take a break and get a life," she continued. I rolled my eyes as I turned back to the paper I'd been staring at.

"I'm Fate, Mia. I have to work so I can give them all the happiness they deserve." I'd held Fate's magic inside me for the last few centuries, and while Fate was responsible for a lot of things, my part of the magic helped people find their mates when I put it to use. All the souls in all the realms depended on me to help them meet their mates. I didn't personally help them all—it was physically impossible, no matter what magic I used. My pixies drew on my magic to pair most people, and until a few years ago, I hadn't really involved myself too much in the work.

Then I'd sensed the birth of the man who would mate with a supe—a supernatural—if I could help him in time. He wasn't the one who interested me the most, though. It was the chain of events his mating led to that caught my attention since one of those *events* included my brother finding his mate. That was when I'd first started getting more involved in my work. Now, after almost a decade living in Mistvale, I couldn't imagine going back to the time when I didn't work every day. There was something extremely fulfilling about helping someone find the happiness they deserved, and I'd quickly grown addicted to the feeling.

"Ugh! What am I for, then? Didn't you create me and the other two thousand pixies so we could do this work for you? Your brother is the king of Afterworld, and even *he* takes weekends off!"

I rolled my eyes at that, chuckling. "Tharion is an idiot, and he doesn't even have a work ethic." I loved my brother dearly, but sometimes I felt like he didn't take his work as seriously as he should. Then again, I'd been just like him until a couple decades ago.

"And *yet*, he gets all his work done and still has a life."

"Hey! I have a life," I protested, finally shutting the file since it was clear I wouldn't be able to get any work done with Mia hovering. Sensing she was winning, Mia perched herself on my desk, her flimsy wings fluttering as she raised a perfectly arched brow.

"You do, huh? Okay, tell me the last time you hung out with someone who isn't family or a pixie? When was the last time you treated yourself to something special?"

"Well, I..." I trailed off as I realized I didn't have an answer.

"Exactly. So now you have two options, and I won't take no for an answer. You'll either take this weekend off and do something fun for yourself, or I'm going to go talk to that dragon friend of yours and tell him and his friends you're lonely and in need of some company."

My eyes widened at the threat, and I stared at her open-mouthed. Mistvale had a really healthy supe population, and most of them had formed one big family who were all up in each other's business in the best of ways. It was the bonds they'd built as a family that had kept me tethered to the town, even after I'd made sure everything would go exactly the way it needed to for everyone. Raiden, a storm dragon I'd accidentally met a few years ago, was the keeper of Mistvale, and though he didn't know what I really was, he'd been trying his best to get me more involved in his family. He'd jump at the chance to drag me into their loving clan. While I loved the people of Mistvale, I maintained a distance from them because I didn't want them to discover who I was. Fate was just a magical entity to the supes, not a person, and I preferred to keep it that way.

"Okay, okay. I'll take the weekend off, but I have absolutely no idea what I can do for myself." And that was true. If I were in Afterworld, I'd probably sit in my favorite gardens for a few hours with a good book. I didn't feel like going to Afterworld today, though. Tharion would probably drag me to one of his weekend beach parties if he found out I was home, and the last thing I wanted was sand in my hair.

"Why don't you check out more of the town? You barely leave your cabin most days. I hear there's a cool shopping center in town called Toss." There was a mischievous glint in Mia's eyes that I didn't quite trust, but I knew she wouldn't lead me toward anything dangerous.

"Toss? What kind of name is that?" I asked as I got to my feet. If I really was taking the day off, there was no point in sitting in my study.

"Well, it's an acronym. TOSS for The One Stop Shops," Mia explained, and I grinned. Mistvalers had a knack for cutesy names.

"Okay, I'll go check this shopping center out. But come Monday, you will let me work without interruption. Agreed?"

Mia gave me a grin that was equal parts mischief and excitement, making my stomach swoop. That look was *never* a good thing. I didn't know where they got it from since they were fragments of *my* magic, but the pixies were a mischievous bunch. I trusted them to carry out their duties, but they also had a habit of stirring up trouble just for the sake of entertainment. Was Mia planning something? And if she was, did I want to know what? Probably not.

"I promise. Oh, and it'll be Christmas soon. I bet the center is all dolled up too! Have some fun, okay? Buy some new clothes, eat some cake..." Her voice trailed off as she flew out of the room, and I shook my head.

As a resident of Afterworld, I didn't really have a fixed physical form. I could take almost any humanoid shape, whether that was a human or vampire or something else. I preferred taking the form of a fae since they had the most androgynous form, and it suited me well on most days, not to mention I'd been one myself in my previous life.

When I felt particularly masc or femme, I could just alter my form accordingly. It was a perk I was grateful for, and I wished I could grant the power to every person out there who had to deal with body dysphoria so they could have the body they felt most comfortable in. Unfortunately, that was something even the all-powerful Fate couldn't do.

With a sigh, I walked over to my closet and riffled through the clothes I had. New clothes and cakes, huh? I could manage that.

Hector

"Come on, Hec! It's almost Christmas. Where's your holiday spirit?" Iris demanded with her usual radiant smile as she slid past me, pulling out a batch of cupcakes from the oven.

I grunted as I went through my spice jars and jotted down the spices that needed refilling. While I loved brewing different teas and offering them at the shop I owned with Iris, being social was not one of my skills. Iris seemed to have some kind of superpower that allowed her to be able to deal with me, but she didn't let me out in front of the customers, and I liked it that way. I was perfectly content brewing my tea blends in the kitchen.

"Hector, come on! Give me a smile! Please?" Iris poked my side, and I sighed heavily to show my annoyance with the perky woman I called my best friend.

With more care than strictly required, I placed my pen on the notepad before turning to look at her. She watched me with wide, expectant eyes, and I blew out a breath. Holding her gaze, I spread my lips in the widest, most maniacal grin I could.

"Holy Jesus fucking Christ, Hector!" Iris swore as she slapped my arm, and I gave a rough chuckle. Well, that's what she got for forcing me to be something I wasn't. I wasn't *smiley*. I didn't enjoy the holidays. Especially Christmas.

For as long as I could remember, Christmas was the day I felt the most alone. Being a foster kid from the age of four meant I grew up listening to kids in school talk about how fun their Christmases were and how many gifts they'd gotten while I hadn't even been lucky enough to get a fucking hug. I envied those kids. I hated those kids. Then I hated the fact that I hated them because most of them were nice to me.

Even now, when I was thirty-two, owned my business, and had a pretty great friend in Iris, those feelings still lingered. All the Christmas decor and happy families made me feel even grumpier. Iris knew that, of course, which was why she was bugging me. She was good at pulling me out of my funks, but I didn't think she'd be any help this time.

"Let me work. Don't you have customers to tend to?" I grumbled as I picked up my pen again. Had I checked the cinnamon?

"It's dead outside, man. Apparently, no one wants cake at eleven in the morning," Iris said, her voice dry. I shook my head as I skirted around her and opened the second spice cabinet, taking stock of the spices I shared with Iris. While I had a cabinet all to myself, we also shared some things that were commonly used across tea and cakes, and as usual, Iris was running low on too much and hadn't thought to alert me.

Grumbling under my breath, I wrote down what I needed to get from the grocery store. They usually had all the common spices we needed, and I ordered the spices that needed to be imported months in advance so I wouldn't run low.

"Ooh, customer! Be right back!" I waved her off, grateful for the reprieve from her constant lurking.

I ignored the voices outside as Iris chatted with the customer and sighed when I finally had the list completed. I'd double-check again before leaving tonight, but for now, I could scratch this task off my to-do list.

"You have kukicha?" The customer's voice was loud with surprise, and I jerked my head up. People rarely ordered kukicha because they either didn't know what it was or they didn't like how low in caffeine it was. Kukicha was one of my favorite blends.

I had a sudden urge to peek out and see who the customer was, maybe tell them how I'd read about it online and given it a try only to realize it was the best tea ever created.

But I stood frozen right where I was because I sucked at talking with customers, and I didn't want them to leave before they gave the tea a try.

"Oh, yes, we do. It's one of Hector's specialties," Iris answered, and I strained to hear what the customer said.

"Oh, I'd love a cup, please. And maybe one of those cookies?"

"Okay, that will be twelve dollars and thirty-eight cents. I'll bring your order to your table in a few."

"Thank you, Iris," the customer said, and I could hear the smile in their voice. They had a pleasant voice, soft and almost melodic.

Wait, what? When did I start describing people's *voices*?

I shook my head and got to work making the tea, the motions familiar and comforting. I'd made kukicha for myself this morning, and while I could re steep the leaves, I went with a fresh spoonful to make it as perfect as possible.

I poured the tea into a cute china cup Iris had picked up from a yard sale a few months ago and placed it on the accompanying saucer just as Iris hurried into the back room.

"Holy damn, Hector," Iris said as she fanned herself, a tray in her hand. She'd already plated one of her special Christmas cookies, and I placed the tea in the empty space.

"What?" I asked as I started cleaning up the area. While it wasn't too messy, Iris was a stickler for keeping the kitchen space spotless, and I'd learned early on to clean up after myself the moment my work was done.

"That had to be the most gorgeous person I've seen this week. Like, oh. Em. Gee."

"I don't think that's how you're supposed to say that." Iris rolled her eyes at me as she headed back toward the front.

"Take a peek, Hector. You won't be disappointed, I promise."

I shook my head as I waved her off, even though part of me wanted to see the customer. Not because of how good looking they were but because of the excitement I'd heard in their voice when they'd asked for kukicha. I wanted to know who else loved the Japanese tea as much as I did.

Feeling like an idiot and unable to resist temptation all the same, I snuck over to the small window that opened into the main store area. I scanned the seating area and spotted Iris smiling down at the customer as she said something. She was twirling her hair around her finger like she did when she was flirting, and I rolled my eyes as I followed her gaze to the customer.

My breath caught in my chest as I took them in. While their clothes would make me think they were female, something told me I'd be wrong. They had dark, russet skin that seemed to glow in the overhead light, and they were smiling as they talked to Iris.

But then they picked up the teacup and wrapped their lips around the rim. I blew out a breath as they took a sip, my eyes locked on their face as their eyes drifted shut. I couldn't hear them from where I stood, but I imagined they hummed at the taste, and goose bumps rose on my arms at how *good* that made me feel.

I didn't know if I made a sound or if it was just a coincidence, but the moment the customer opened their eyes, they turned their head just a little, and just like that, I was gazing into a pair of pale green eyes, trapped.

I jerked away from the window, my heart pounding in my chest. Fuck. Fuck. Fuck. *Way to creep them out, Hector.*

I slumped against the counter and buried my face in my palms as I groaned loudly, my thoughts inexplicable mush.

Would the customer ever come back after that horror show? I hoped they would. If they did, I'd pull up my big boy pants and apologize to them.

TWO

Celeste

The first thought that crossed my mind when I spotted the man staring at me through the tiny window behind the counter was that he was a creep. But then I found myself unable to look away from his dark gaze and my magic stirred inside me.

It took me a moment to realize what was happening, why my heart wanted me to rush into that kitchen and drag the man back home with me. *Mate.* He was my mate.

I shook my head as I tried to clear the fog from my mind and realized the man had disappeared. Fuck.

He was my mate. Was that why Mia had sent me to TOSS? She'd even mentioned getting some cake. She'd wanted me to go to the bakery.

How had I not sensed it? I was the one who paired everyone. Shouldn't I have realized my mate was near? Those scheming pixies!

"You okay?" Iris asked, and I looked up at the witch, giving her a smile.

"Yes. Yes, I am. Just... Was that your partner in there? Dark eyes, light stubble?" That was all I'd seen of the man.

"Oh my god, was he peeking through the window?" she asked with a laugh as she shot a glance back at the store. "I think he was curious about the person who ordered his favorite tea. Few do."

"Oh," I said with a nod, wondering if he was a human or a supe. I hadn't been able to sense it, but since Iris was a witch, I supposed I could ask her. "Um, is he a supe?"

Iris tilted her head from side to side. "Yeah. He's an alchemist, but he doesn't use his skills for anything except his tea blends."

That made sense, I guessed. We were long past the time when alchemists created the most lethal—and undetectable—poisons for the right price. Otherworld's Anubis Squad—the supernatural police, for want of a better term—had shut that practice down decades ago.

"Could you please tell him the kukicha was absolutely delightful? It was even better than the one I had in Japan."

Iris laughed softly as she pushed her strawberry-blond hair back. It fell forward again when she nodded and said, "I will, though I don't think his ego needs any more inflating."

I smiled as I stood up and took a step back from my chair. I hadn't shopped for any clothes yet, but now I had a reason to. I had someone to impress and to pull out of that room he was hiding in.

"Thank you for the tea and cookie. And the conversation," I said, and Iris smiled.

"It was my pleasure. Hey, can I ask what your pronouns are? I'm pretty sure Hector is going to ask me questions about you, and I don't want to use the wrong ones."

I felt a flutter in my belly at the thought of my mate talking or even thinking about me, and I smiled. *His name was Hector.* "I'm always okay with they/them pronouns." Some days I felt more like using he or she pronouns, but even then, they/them didn't bother me.

"Perfect, thank you. I hope you'll visit again, Celeste."

"I'm sure I will." *Very, very sure.*

I walked out of the tea shop and bit my lip as I took in the clothing stores. Mistvale didn't have any of the big name stores, which I loved, but I didn't think Threads & Needles would have the kind of clothing I preferred. I could always use my magic to change them, but something about the idea of sifting through clothes in a legitimate store until I found something *just perfect* appealed to me right then.

I spotted a store that looked more like a high-end boutique and smiled. Wish for It looked like it was just what I needed. A plaque at the door read, *Make your request with the words* I wish, *and it shall be fulfilled.*

I chuckled at the sign, but the moment I stepped into the store, I realized I was in the company of another supe, and the sign wasn't as gimmicky as I'd assumed. I glanced at the counter where a Middle Eastern man stood staring at something I couldn't see. He broke out of his reverie when I walked into the store and gave me a faint smile.

"Welcome to Wish for It. I'm Kezan. What can I do for you?" A djinn, I realized, and a moment later, the threads of his destiny unfurled in my mind. The poor man had suffered enough, but he'd have to wait another few years before he would find his mate. I hated making them wait, but the threads were complicated, and I had to be careful. Getting them tangled would cause consequences much worse than a few years' wait. I had to take all kinds of circumstances into consideration, and if I pushed Kezan's mate toward him before they were both ready, it would only result in heartbreak and a broken bond.

"Um, I wish to find clothes that match my style," I said, waving at the deep red silk gown I wore in explanation. Heads had turned throughout the shopping center when they saw me, and while I didn't particularly want to stick out, I hated the idea of not being myself even more. I'd gotten used to the freedom I had in Afterworld.

I felt a faint buzz of magic run through the store. The djinn had imbued the entire store with his magic. That was nifty.

"I think I know just what you need," he said as he led me toward a rack full of all kinds of outfits, all made from silk. Had this been there already, or did the magic create it just for me?

Shaking my head, I smiled at him. "Thank you so much. These look wonderful."

Kezan nodded as he took a step back. "I'll leave you to it. Please let me know if you need any assistance."

I spent the next hour picking through gowns and dresses and random shirts that caught my eye before finally settling on three gowns, two dresses, and a pair of silk pants that I just couldn't resist.

Kezan smiled as I brought everything to the counter, though his eyes were red-rimmed. I knew what caused it, of course. His threads had told me everything about him, including the fact that he'd just lost the keeper of his bottle. He was grieving, and yet there he was working in the shop that had been his keeper's dream. He was a good man, and he deserved someone who would treat him well. I'd make sure he found him.

Sometimes being able to see the threads seemed more like a curse to me, especially at times like these when I desperately wanted to do something but couldn't. It was why I used to spend most of my time in Afterworld. The souls in Afterworld had either already found their mates or were waiting to be reborn, in which case they would only find their mates once they were back in the human realm. It was easier to live there, but I didn't regret moving to the human realm, though I wondered if it was time to move back home now that I'd found my mate.

Kezan billed me with quiet efficiency, and I didn't strike up a conversation because I sensed he needed silence. Once I had my clothes, I waved him goodbye before walking out of the store.

Kezan would find his mate when he was ready for it. For now, I needed to figure out how to woo my own mate.

Pairing others sounded so much easier now.

Hector

Iris rushed into the kitchen area a few minutes later, and I looked at her from where I was moping on the floor, my back leaning against the counter. I couldn't believe I'd done something so idiotic.

"What the hell are you doing down there, Hec?" she asked with a laugh, and I groaned.

"Regretting my choices," I grumbled as I got to my feet, dusting off my clothes even though I knew the kitchen was almost clinically clean.

I washed my hands at the sink as Iris chuckled, trying my best to ignore her. "Well, they are mighty fine, aren't they? I'd love to get my hands all over them," Iris said with a sigh, and I rolled my eyes.

"You'd love to get your hands on ninety percent of the adult population," I snarked, and she chuckled again.

"Nothing wrong with loving 'em all. I just have too much love in my heart. I wish I could lend some of it to you so you could turn your heart back from the stone it has turned to," she teased, and I shook my head. I wanted to ask her about the customer, but I didn't want her to realize just how curious I was about them. The moment Iris sensed I had even a bit of interest in someone, she made it her mission to get me to date them, which didn't go well. Ever.

"Guess what they told me?" Iris asked, and I knew she was talking about the tea customer. I raised a brow at her so she'd continue, hoping she couldn't see just how interested I really was.

"They told me to tell you the tea was *delightful* and better than some they had in Japan. They also caught you peeking at them like a creep, so there's that." I turned beet red at the mention of my embarrassment and turned my attention to my notepad, doodling in the corner to avoid looking at Iris. "I think someone's interested in someone."

"No, I'm not," I answered hastily, and Iris giggled. She walked over to me and squished me into a hug, resting her chin on my shoulder. I sighed gustily because I knew trying to pull away would just prompt her to squeeze me tighter.

"I actually meant Celeste. They seemed very curious about you, but now I can see it isn't one-sided, and I'm thrilled."

"Well, you're wrong," I grumbled as I tried to pull away from the hug while my heart was trying to jump out of my chest at the thought that Celeste was interested in me.

I shook my head as I blew out a sigh. Even if I was interested, I didn't know what I would do about it. I didn't know how to get close to anyone. After being burned so many times,

I'd forgotten how the whole thing was done. I wasn't sure I wanted to try. The only reason Iris and I were as close as we were was because she didn't know how to give up.

Why the hell was I thinking about this anyway? I'd just served them a cup of tea—and stared at them like a creep—and this wasn't the start of some holiday romance.

A customer showed up out front and Iris finally let me go, hurrying out of the kitchen to take care of their order. I took in a deep breath and blew it out slowly. I needed to focus on my work and nothing else.

As I lay in bed that night, I looked around the bare room and wondered if I should've decorated for Christmas. What was the point when it would be just me like always? I had the yearly dinner at Iris's place with her parents, but other than that, I had no holiday plans.

I wondered if things would be different if I had a partner. Would they have insisted we decorate? Would we have spent a whole day setting up a tree and decorating it with special ornaments that told a story?

As exhausting as it sounded, I realized I would've enjoyed doing all of that with someone. Getting passed around from one foster family to another, I'd never really gotten a chance to experience Christmas like they showed on TV. The closest was the year I'd spent with my last foster family—Iris's parents—when they'd included me in their family celebration like I actually belonged.

I imagined getting a tree straight from the farm at the edge of town. Maybe my partner and I would cut down our favorite tree ourselves. We'd bring it home and put it up in my cramped living room to brighten it up a little. We'd make stupid paper ornaments as some cheesy holiday movie played in the background. The air would be thick with the scent of baked goodies we'd feast on the whole day.

As I kept imagining the fanciful scenario, my faceless partner turned to the intriguing person I'd seen today. Celeste. I watched them as they raised up on their toes to put a golden star at the top of the tree, the colorful beads in their braids tinkling softly as they turned to smile widely at me, proud of their accomplishment.

I watched as they walked closer to me, our heights the same with the heels they wore. I reached out and took one of their braids between my thumb and index finger, pulling it closer. Everything about them was fascinating, and I took in everything from their rich hair to their dark, russet skin that almost seemed to glow. Their green eyes were lit from within, and once I met them, I couldn't look away.

I didn't know when I fell asleep, but hours later, when I woke up warm and cozy, I had a smile on my face and a fluttery feeling in my chest I had no name for.

THREE

Celeste

"I can't believe you did that. Why didn't you tell me I'd be meeting my mate? Come to think of it, why didn't I know I'd find my mate there?" I demanded as Mia fluttered just out of reach.

After making me visit the bakery—and therefore my mate—Mia had disappeared for three days straight. I'd visited the shop every day, though I hadn't tried to talk to Hector yet because I'd been trying to come up with a game plan. It seemed like he was either shy or not very social, so I needed some way to make him trust me, some way to show him he didn't need to hide from me.

I'd had the perfect idea last night, and I'd woken up and gotten dressed in a hurry, almost forgetting I had an appointment with Niall that morning.

I worked as a therapist, which my brother teased me about incessantly since he couldn't imagine why I'd want to spend even more time helping others when I already did so much as Fate. But this was a different type of work, and I enjoyed making the lives of these people just a little easier. Niall Rodgers was my favorite client—even though I wasn't supposed to pick favorites—and like all my patients, he was a supernatural, a vampire. I didn't have any formal education in the field, but I understood people in a way few others could, and since supes couldn't very well visit human therapists, I tried to help them the best I could.

After I'd spent an hour with Niall, we were both satisfied with his progress. He didn't really need these sessions anymore, but talking over his month comforted him, so we had an hour-long session every month.

With Niall gone, I'd been ready to rush out the door when Mia had shown up. Since I needed answers from her as well, I decided waiting another few minutes would change nothing.

"Well... I don't know why you didn't know. Probably because you only ever worry about others? When was the last time you looked at your own threads?"

She wasn't wrong. I couldn't remember the last time I'd read my own threads, but I focused on them now, and there it was, my thread crossing another and then intertwining with it for the rest of eternity.

"I was hoping you'd see it and start looking for him, but when you didn't, I decided I needed to step in. Aren't you glad I did?" Mia asked with a self-satisfied smirk.

"I am, I am. Thank you, Mia." I smiled up at her, and she winked.

"I'll take care of everything for the next few weeks. You focus on wooing your mate, all right?"

I chuckled as I shook my head. "I was just about to head to the bakery, actually."

"Oh my god, don't tell me you're going to stalk your mate like King Damien did. You remember how long it took him to get together with his mates, right? Two years! I ain't doing your work for two years, Fate or not!"

I laughed at that. Poor Damien would forever be known for his stalking tendencies it seemed. "I don't plan on stalking Hector. Don't worry. I have a plan."

"Phew. Okay, then. Shoo, off you go, Your Highness," she gave me a low bow before doing a roll in midair.

"Cut the sass, Mia," I said as I walked by her, poking her in the belly as I went.

Mia hissed but did nothing, and I smiled as I walked out of the cabin I called home. I could easily teleport to TOSS, but there was never a guarantee I wouldn't be spotted since there weren't any deserted spaces around the center.

Plus, I enjoyed driving most of the time. It wasn't like I had a reason to drive in Afterworld, so when I got the chance to do it in the human realm, I took it.

When I arrived at the tea and sweets shop called She Bakes He Brews, I found Iris behind the counter. I had a feeling Hector rarely interacted with the customers. I hadn't even seen his face yet, not properly, but I was so caught up in him already. Was this how it was for the people I paired up? It felt weird to be on the other side. Weird and wonderful.

"Hey, Celeste! What can I get you today?" Iris asked in a bright, cheerful voice, and I glanced at the board that listed all the teas they offered. I smiled when I found the perfect blend for today's plan.

"I'll take a rooibos latte, please. Is it okay if I wait here for it?"

"Of course! Let me just pass your order along to Hector," Iris said, and I stopped her before she could leave.

"Can you please tell him to take his time? I know good rooibos tastes better when steeped for a long time, and I'm in no hurry."

Iris grinned as if she saw through my plan and knew exactly what I was up to. Thankfully, she didn't say anything. She stuck her head through the kitchen door and told Hector my order before returning to her post.

"He said fifteen minutes tops," Iris said. Her eyes flicked up and down, taking me in, and I knew what she was about to ask. "Are your pronouns... "

"He and him," I answered with a half smile. I'd dressed in a button-down, leggings, and heels, so I imagined she was confused. "Actually, I have this magical aura that would always tell you my correct pronouns if you wouldn't mind me using it? I don't use it much in this realm, but you're both supes." I immediately regretted my words when Iris's eyes widened and she leaned forward, palms braced on the counter top.

"Wait, so it's true? There really is a fae realm?" she demanded. Fuck! I'd actually meant Otherworld and Afterworld, but it wasn't like I could tell her about that. People of the human realm—supes or otherwise—weren't supposed to know about the other realms. While the Faerie realm existed, I had no idea where it was. No one except the Fae knew. Fae were notoriously good with their illusions, and they kept their realm hidden at all times. Even though I'd been a fae in my previous life, I was no longer one and therefore had no access to that realm.

"I can neither confirm nor deny that." I settled on a diplomatic answer, and Iris rolled her eyes.

"Let me guess? You'd tell me, but then you'd have to kill me, right?"

I laughed at the smirk on her face and shook my head. "Something like that." *More like you have to die before you can see Otherworld*, I thought.

Hector

I sprinkled some powdered cinnamon on the concoction, smiling at the perfect rooibos latte. I knew little about the person standing outside other than the fact that he had great taste in tea, and yet I couldn't help but want to know more, which was something that didn't happen often with me.

I'd been listening to their conversation as I made the tea, and the change in his pronouns made me curious about the aura thing he'd mentioned. I'd never heard of such a thing, but then again, I'd never met a fae before. I was thirty-two, a baby by supe standards. The only other supes I'd met other than Iris were the patrons who visited the shop, and even then, I'd rarely talked to them. I wasn't a people person, which was why I slid Celeste's latte through the little kitchen window instead of going out and offering it to him like a part of me wanted to. A tiny, hopeful part of me that I squashed quickly.

I hurried over to the door when Iris picked up the mug and pressed my ear to it, leaning closer so I could hear what Celeste said. Would he like the latte? Had I made it too sweet? What if he didn't like vanilla?

"Oh, wait!" Iris said, and I wondered why she'd said that when the door opened outward and I tumbled into the shop area. Fuck!

"Hector!" Iris gasped as she helped me up. My cheeks warmed as an embarrassed blush raced up my neck, and I swallowed hard as I looked at the person who had me feeling things I'd never felt before. My first look at him had been hasty and through a tiny window that didn't allow for much examination.

But now I found myself caught in the most beautiful green eyes I'd ever seen. They were pale, almost gray, with a ring of darker green at the edge of his pupils.

It took me a few long moments to break away from his mesmerizing gaze, and I bit my lip as I turned to Iris. "Sorry about that. I slipped." She knew I was lying, but she didn't say anything, which I was grateful for.

I turned back and opened the kitchen door, ready to escape back into my safe space, when Celeste spoke. "Hector, wait!" My name sounded so different on his lips, so much better. I couldn't stop myself from turning slightly so I could look at him, though I kept hold of the door handle.

Celeste played with one of his braids as he looked at me. For a moment, he looked nervous and uncertain. Then he smiled, and the look disappeared, making me wonder if I'd imagined it. "Would you like to go out with me sometime this week?"

My eyes widened at the question. That was the last thing I'd expected him to say. Correction: I hadn't expected him to say anything remotely close to that. "I'm sorry. I can't," I blurted out as I slipped back into the kitchen, slamming the door shut behind me. Fuck. Fuck. Fuck.

I had zero experience with these things, but I knew I'd royally fucked up. He'd looked so earnest, and I'd just shot him down. Why? Because I was scared? Because I didn't know what he'd seen in me to ask me out?

Hell, we'd never even properly met. He'd seen me creeping on him through the window and again today through the door—there was no way he believed my lie—and the first thing he'd done was ask me out? It made no sense.

Still, I could've been gentler in rejecting him, right? I wished I was brave enough to say yes to him, but I wasn't.

"What the fuck, Hec?" Iris demanded as she stepped into the room, and I assumed Celeste had left. Shit. Had he even drunk the latte I'd made him?

I spotted the empty mug in Iris's hand and relaxed a little, a warm feeling fluttering deep in my belly despite everything.

"What?" I asked as if I didn't know what she was talking about.

"Why did you reject him? I know you're interested too, so don't bullshit me." She looked really disappointed, which was weird because as often as she tried setting me up, she never minded if I said no. She would just say something like, "You'll be ready someday, just you wait," and let it go. It didn't seem like that would happen today.

"I... I don't know," I mumbled. I didn't want to tell her I was scared. I was scared that if I ever let myself care for someone, they'd throw me away after a while like so many of my foster families had. I never wanted to feel like that again. Disposable. Exchangeable. Like I had no value. Being alone was a lot better than feeling worthless.

Iris and her family were the only ones who had ever wanted me around. My birth parents hadn't, my foster families hadn't, and my one try at a relationship hadn't wanted me for more than a few fucks either. It was better to stay alone. I had Iris and her family. That was enough. It had to be enough.

"Is it because he's genderfluid?" Iris asked, and I glared at her, honestly offended she'd say something like that.

"Of course not. I don't care what gender he is or what's in his pants," I grumbled. Celeste was perfect. He was beautiful, mesmerizing, and magical. Any guy would be lucky to have him as his partner. It just couldn't be me.

"Then what?" Iris asked as she walked closer. "You know I've never pushed you to give someone a chance, Hec, but I really think Celeste would be good for you. I saw the way he looked at you. Hell, I saw the way you looked at him. What's stopping you ? Tell me, please?" Iris placed her arms on my shoulders, and I looked at her. She was a few inches taller than me because of her heels, but right then, I felt even smaller.

"I'm scared," I whispered softly. "I'm scared of being discarded again."

Iris's eyes widened, and I looked away, not wanting her to see how deep that feeling went for me.

"Oh, sweetie," she murmured as she pulled me into a hug, her arms warm and familiar around me. For just a moment, I let myself sink into the comfort she offered, wishing I wasn't like this.

I wished I could give Celeste the chance he deserved. If only I wasn't such a coward…

FOUR

Celeste

I knew I shouldn't have eavesdropped, but I needed to know why Hector had said no. Was it something I'd done, or was it something outside my control?

I'd been leaving the food court when I'd remembered I could turn incorporeal in the human realm if I wanted to. Somehow, I'd found myself in an empty nook where I'd ditched my corporeal form before sneaking back to the shop.

Iris had been heading into the back room when I got there, so I'd slipped in with her without a problem.

I'm scared of being discarded again. Hector's words had been filled with so much pain, and a part of me wanted to hunt down the people who had made him feel that way, which was surprising since I detested violence.

"You know you'll always have me, Mom, and Dad, right?" Iris murmured, and Hector nodded against her. I was glad he had someone in his corner, and it was clear Iris really cared about him.

"Honey, you'll find someone who treasures you for the prize you are. I just know it. But you need to take a chance, you know? I'm not saying go out with Celeste tomorrow, but maybe open yourself to the idea of giving things a try."

"I'll try, Iris. But don't expect me to get over it in a day," Hector grumbled, and I almost smiled.

I realized I needed a different plan. I needed to slow down even more. Instead of trying to date Hector, I had to win his trust first.

As I drove home, I thought about what I could do to make Hector see he was the one for me, that I would be there for him as long as he wanted if he'd only let me in.

At home, I hurried into my study since that was where my mind worked the best and focused on the problem. Somehow, I had to win Hector's trust, but how would I do that when he wouldn't even come out in front of me?

My eyes fell on the notepad on my desk, and an idea formed in my head. I grabbed the notepad and a pen before heading to the living room. I sank into my comfy armchair, grabbing the silk shawl from the back and draping it over my lap.

Blowing out a breath, I started to write.

Dear Hector...

When I finished writing, I realized I wasn't alone. I looked up to find Mia looking at the letter, her small palms pressed to her mouth, her eyes shining. When she found me watching her, she shook her head. "Oh my gosh, I didn't know you wrote so beautifully! Your mate will definitely fall in love with you when he reads it."

I rolled my eyes at her as I folded the letter and placed it on my coffee table, using the snow globe there as a paperweight.

"What's the status of Firey and his mate?" I asked. The cute dolphin shifter had caught my eye when I'd been tracking down the warlock I needed to find for some... future plans. I'd made sure the warlock came to Mistvale so his sister and the dolphin shifter could both find their mates. While the sister had quickly claimed her mate, Firey was being... hesitant.

"Still the same. He watches his mate from afar but never speaks to him. If only he'd ask someone what species his mate is, he'd realize why the man hasn't noticed he's his mate," Mia said with a shake of her head, and I chuckled. Our task was to make sure the mates crossed paths, but after that, they were responsible for their own destinies. It was why it annoyed me whenever someone asked if their mate only loved them because Fate wanted them to.

I didn't want anyone to love anyone if they didn't want to. All I did was make sure people had a chance to meet that one person—and recognize them, in the case of supes—who could be their perfect match. Some people met their mates in their first life in the human realm while others found them in Otherworld. Rarely, souls would find their mates in Afterworld—the realm humans had tried to replicate in their idea of heaven.

"Well, we did our jobs. Now it's up to those two to make it work," I said with a shrug. The supes of Mistvale interested me a lot, which was why I spent half my time in this realm. Before I'd come across Jai and Raphael's threads, I'd done all my work from Afterworld. Now, I couldn't imagine not getting to see the fruits of my labor. I loved watching mates find love with each other.

"That's true. As for the Otherworld men..." Mia trailed off with a grin, and I shook my head. Their threads told me the men of Otherworld would come across their mates amidst dangerous times, but since I wasn't an oracle, I couldn't determine exactly where the danger would come from. I'd warned the king of Otherworld and my brother—the king of Afterworld—regardless, but I wished I could do more.

"Anyway, what's he like?" Mia asked, and when I gave her a puzzled look, she clarified, "Your mate. What's he like?"

I smiled as I thought of Hector. The way he'd tumbled into the shop today. I'd barely held back my laugh, but the adorable blush on his face had made it hard not to smile. Then the way he'd held my eyes, his brown ones so full of conflicting feelings.

"He's... he's amazing. But he's scared. I need to win his trust first." I didn't understand what life had been like for him. I'd never felt like I could be discarded or that I was disposable. I was Fate, and people *always* needed me.

I wasn't arrogant about it, or at least I hoped I wasn't. I enjoyed helping people, and I liked being wanted. I couldn't relate to Hector. What I could do was make him see he was important to me. I wanted him in my life, and I'd never not want him.

"All right, back to work. Let me know if you need any help."

"Sir, yes, sir!" Mia said with a mock salute, and I chuckled as she flew away.

With a sigh, I grabbed the letter and stood up. Tomorrow, I'd give it to Hector and hope he didn't shred it and dump it without reading it.

Hector

I yawned for the hundredth time that morning as I donned my apron and got ready for the day. I felt like I might need it today with how clumsy I was being. Lack of sleep would do that, I supposed.

Last night, all I'd been able to think about was Celeste. Hell, who was I kidding? I was still thinking about him.

I couldn't believe how abrupt I'd been with him. I should apologize, shouldn't I? Tell him I hadn't said no because of him. My own issues had fucked up my chance with him. Celeste was... well, he was very close to perfect.

"Stop daydreaming, Hector. Your kettle is screaming," Iris said, and I jumped as I realized she was right. I hurried over to it and took it off the stove, pouring the piping hot water into a mug to make a strong cup of tea for myself. I needed all the caffeine I could get.

"Sorry," I mumbled, avoiding her eyes the best I could. Iris knew me better than anyone else, and if she started asking questions, I didn't think I'd be able to focus at all.

Thankfully, a customer arrived before she could chew me out, and I busied myself with work as I wondered if Celeste would avoid the shop now. Would he go somewhere else for his daily tea? The thought was disappointing, and I shook it off.

It was an hour later that I heard his voice, and I bit my lip as I glanced at my special tea leaves, wondering what he'd order today. A purple tea maybe?

"Order for you. A green tea with no sugar," Iris said as she stuck her head into the room, and I stopped short. A green tea? "Oh, and here," she held something out to me, and I took it from her without looking at it, my mind too caught up with the fact that something had definitely changed. Celeste didn't want to try my special blends anymore. Was it because of what happened yesterday? What a stupid question, of course it was because of that.

It was only after I'd reached my workspace that I looked down and saw what Iris had handed me. It was a folded sheet of paper with the words For Hector written in a beautiful, cursive script on one side.

I unfolded it, biting my lip when I saw the signature at the end. Celeste had written me a letter.

His handwriting was beautiful, just like him, and I flattened the paper before I started reading.

Dear Hector,

I wanted to apologize for yesterday. I realize I may have come on too strong. I'm sorry I surprised you, and please know I'm not at all hurt over the rejection. Disappointed maybe, but I understand where you were coming from.

We haven't even had a real conversation yet, so I suppose it was stupid of me to do what I did. Can we have a do-over, please?

I'd like to get to know you, even if it never leads to a relationship. If you're agreeable to that, could you please make me a yerba mate tea instead? And maybe share your number with me so we could talk? I would have shared mine, but I didn't want to be presumptuous.

I would really love to get to know you, Hector. I haven't been able to stop thinking about you since I first saw you, and I'd be honored if you gave me a chance.

Take care,

Celeste

I read the letter twice before I carefully folded it and stuck it into my back pocket.

Could I? Could I give Celeste a chance? He'd asked for friendship. I could do friendship, right? I hadn't been able to stop thinking about him either, so that was another reason to give it a chance.

I remembered what Iris had said yesterday. I needed to at least try.

Decision made, I grabbed the tea leaves I needed and got to work. This tea was pretty simple to make, and I had Celeste's cup ready to serve a few minutes later.

I glanced at my notepad and bit my lip before carefully tearing off a small, rectangular piece of paper—frayed edges unnerved me big time—and jotting down my number on it. Then, I folded the piece of paper and stuck it between the cup and saucer before passing it through the window.

A moment later, Iris's head appeared in the doorway again, her brows furrowed. "Are you okay? Do you feel unwell?"

"Huh? No, I'm fine. Why?" I asked as I wiped down the counter to avoid thinking about what I'd just done.

"Well, you gave me the wrong tea for Celeste, and that's never happened before," Iris said, and I realized she was still holding the cup. She hadn't given it to Celeste yet?

"Don't worry. It's the one he wants. Trust me," I said with a smile, and Iris gave me a puzzled look before shrugging and leaving with the tea.

"Please don't make me regret this, Celeste," I mumbled softly as I glanced at the closed door.

FIVE

Celeste

I stared at the contact page like I had been for the past hour. *Hector a.k.a Mate*. It was cheesy, but I couldn't stop myself from adding the last bit. I'd added his number to my contacts the moment I'd left the shop, but I still hadn't texted him anything.

I wondered if he was waiting for my text. I didn't want him to think I hadn't been serious, though, so I clicked on the text button and typed out a brief message, quickly sending it so I wouldn't be tempted to ponder it for another ten minutes.

Me: Hey, Hector. It's Celeste.

Hector a.k.a Mate: Hey, Celeste.

I wondered if Hector was just as awkward over text as he was face-to-face, and the thought made me smile. Quickly, I typed another text.

Me: I really am sorry for what I did yesterday.

Hector a.k.a Mate: I have no idea why you asked me out, but it wasn't your fault. If it weren't for my hang-ups, I think I would've said yes.

I smiled at that. Even though he'd said that to Iris yesterday, hearing it straight from him made it even more real.

Me: Would you like me to tell you why I asked you out? Or would you rather we forget it ever happened?

Hector a.k.a Mate: I really want to know why, but I don't want to sound like I'm fishing for compliments.

I chuckled at that, shaking my head. Remembering yesterday, I looked around to make sure Mia wasn't peeking at my texts, but she wasn't there. Phew.

Me: I don't mind telling you. I know we haven't really talked before this, but something about you caught my eye. Then there is the tea you make. You had me at that cup of kukicha the first day, and every tea after that just made me want to know you more. The glimpses I caught of you also made me really curious about you. Plus, you're very much my type. There's also something else, but I'm worried I'll scare you off if I say it.

It took him a moment to answer, which was expected considering the essay I'd written. I didn't regret it because he needed to see how special he was. Maybe knowing he was my mate would give him the security he needed to trust in me, to trust in us.

Hector a.k.a Mate: Unless you planned to take me to a cabin in the woods and chop me up, I don't think anything would scare me.

So he was going to ignore all the compliments, was he? Fine by me.

Me: Well, I do have a cabin, but it isn't in the woods. And no, no chopping you up. It's something important, and I'll tell you, but only if you agree you'll still give me a chance.

Hector a.k.a Mate: I'm not sure I can promise that, but I'll try my best. Please don't keep secrets from me.

I blew out a breath as I read his text. I was keeping so many secrets from everyone constantly. But I knew once our bond was complete, I wouldn't keep any secrets from him.

Me: There are some other things that I can only tell you face-to-face, but they don't pertain to our relationship. What does, though, is the fact that you're my mate.

He didn't reply right away, and I wondered if I'd scared him. I should've waited to tell him. Why did I keep getting ahead of myself when it came to him?

I knew why. I'd waited a long time for my mate, all while I was helping others find their mates and watching them live happily. Now that I had someone of my own, I wanted him in my arms as soon as I could have him.

Hector a.k.a Mate: Are you sure?

Me: Very. Did I scare you?

Hector a.k.a Mate: Quite the opposite, actually. I'm kinda relieved to be honest.

Me: I need to confess something.

I regretted it the moment I sent the message, but I knew I needed to tell him. I'd watched a lot of relationships almost fail because of stupid misunderstandings, and I had no plans to let something like that happen. Plus, he'd asked me not to keep secrets from him, and I needed to respect his wishes.

Hector a.k.a Mate: What is it?

Me: I may have eavesdropped on your conversation with Iris after the debacle yesterday. I just wanted to know what I did wrong because you're my mate, and I knew I'd keep trying until you gave in, but I wanted to do it without hurting you, so I needed to know why you'd said no so I could change it.

Hector a.k.a Mate: Oh.

Me: I'm so sorry. I know it was wrong, and I'm sorry I did it. I just... I thought it might have been because of my fluidity, and I needed to know.

Hector a.k.a Mate: Um, it's okay. It wasn't about that. You know that, right? I have absolutely zero problems with it. You look equally beautiful in a gown and in button-downs.

My cheeks warmed at the text. Was he flirting, or was he just trying to convince me he didn't mind?

Me: My magic allows me to take on a male or female form on days I'm feeling particularly masc or femme, but if you'd prefer I stay in my masc form, I can.

It wouldn't be the most comfortable, but I'd do it for him. Then again, I didn't know what his sexuality was, so he might be okay with it.

Hector a.k.a Mate: Please don't do that. I want you to be true to yourself, okay? You don't need to change for me or anyone.

Me: Sorry, I'm getting ahead of myself again, aren't I? I promised I wanted to be friends, and yet I keep bringing relationship stuff into the conversation.

Hector a.k.a Mate: I don't mind. If we're mates, that's where we'll end up anyway, right?

I smiled at the text and had the strangest urge to hug my phone.

Me: Right.

Hector

Celeste was my mate. The fact brought me a sense of relief, and I knew exactly why. If I was Celeste's mate, they'd never give up on me, never abandon me. If I was their mate, I could take a chance on them without the risk of getting my heart broken when they decided to give me up like everyone else had. They wouldn't ever stop caring about me because they were my mate. They'd love me and want me with the same dedication I knew I was capable of if I only let myself feel the things I'd always kept buried to keep myself safe.

The knowledge gave me a freedom I'd always wished for but never had— the freedom to let my guard down and feel. I knew how strong fated mates' bonds were. I had seen it with my own eyes in Iris's parents. They loved each other more than anyone I'd ever met, and I knew they would do anything to avoid ever getting separated. If I could have something even remotely similar to their relationship, I knew I'd be happy. And the idea of having something like that with Celeste? I couldn't even imagine.

After our chat, I spent a long time mulling over things as a steady hope flared deep in my chest. When morning came after a fitful sleep full of anxiety and a strange excitement I'd never felt before, I'd made my decision.

Me: Would you like to hang out with me today?

I put the phone away and took care of my morning routine so I wouldn't be tempted to stare at the screen until a reply came, and when I came back from my shower, I had a message waiting for me.

Celeste: Hang out? In person?

Me: Yes. I have to buy gifts for Iris and her parents, so I thought maybe we could do it together and get to know each other better? If you'd like to, of course.

Celeste: Yes, please.

I smiled at their quick reply and glanced at the time before replying.

Me: Can you come by the shop around noon? We can do the shopping around TOSS and maybe have some tea after.

Celeste: Will I get to watch you make tea?

Watch me make tea? Why would they want to do that? Maybe they wanted to learn.

Me: You want to watch me make tea?

Celeste: Oh yes. I'd love to watch.

Me: Sure, why not. So noon?

Celeste: I'll be there.

I smiled at the text before putting my phone away and getting ready for work. Had I just asked Celeste out on a date, or were we just hanging out as friends?

I rolled my eyes at myself and shook my head as a familiar caw sounded outside my kitchen window. My small house was the last in a line of cul-de-sacs and butted up against Silent Creek Park.

I grabbed the packet of bread pieces and opened the kitchen window into my backyard. Six ravens were scattered around the small backyard. Aja, the bravest—and sassiest—of them flew to the windowsill, and I rolled my eyes as I scratched under his beak.

I'd moved into this house almost ten years ago, and the birds had adopted me during my first year there. According to the internet, ravens lived ten to fifteen years, and these six had stuck by me for the last nine. They followed me to work sometimes, but most days they showed up in the morning for their daily treat before disappearing for the day.

I checked their legs, noting that none of them had lost the tiny bracelets I had made for them. They were a way for me to identify them, and the birds loved shiny things, so I guessed I'd hoped they would know I cared about them if I gave them something shiny.

Who knew how much of my gestures they understood, but I was ridiculously attached to the black birds.

"All right, I need to head to work soon, so be quick, okay?" I grabbed a piece of bread and flung it out the window. Bas swooped down from a tree, catching it in his beak before flying off to another tree and chomping down on it.

I fed them like that until my bag was empty. Then I gave Aja one last scratch beneath his beak before waving them off. I closed the window—I still remembered the horror show my kitchen had turned into the one time I'd left it open, and I didn't want a repeat of that—and grabbed my phone and keys, my thoughts returning to Celeste.

It wasn't a date, was it?

My breath caught in my chest when I stepped out of the kitchen area and found Celeste waiting for me. It was the first time I could actually see them properly and take my time with it. They wore a gorgeous pale gold gown, the smooth silk wrapping beautifully around their slim frame. Golden eye shadow made their green eyes pop, and their lips curved into a smile the moment our eyes met.

I felt under dressed beside them, but I didn't think I could ever match up to even a tenth of their beauty, and I didn't want to. Celeste was unique and the most beautiful person I'd ever laid eyes on.

Now that we were face-to-face with no barriers between us, I could sense the bond. It had a low thrum to it, and it was weak, but I knew it would get stronger the more we got to know each other. I couldn't wait.

"Hey, Hector. You ready to go?"

I couldn't make my voice work, so I nodded. Then I kept standing there, looking at them, until Iris elbowed me in the ribs. "Ow." I rubbed at the abused spot as Celeste bit back a grin. Shaking my head, I walked around the counter and stepped up to Celeste. "You look... magical." I blushed at my dorky comment, but they didn't seem to mind.

Celeste smiled widely as their eyes roamed over me, taking me in. "You look stunning as well, Hector."

"Go, you two. I don't want to see more of this mush here. Shoo." Iris waved us off with a grin, and I rolled my eyes at her. I opened the door for Celeste, and they shot me another smile as they stepped out into the main shopping center.

We'd only walked a few steps when a voice stopped us. "Excuse me, are you a man or a woman?" I narrowed my eyes as Celeste turned around, following their gaze to a young man and woman who were giving them an ill-disguised grimace as if the fact that their measly brains couldn't fathom Celeste's beauty was Celeste's fault.

I opened my mouth to tell them exactly how many undetectable poisons I knew how to make when Celeste squeezed my hand, their grip warm and calming. Then, they turned to the couple and gave them a wide smile. "Aww, did one of you want to ask me out? Thankfully, I already have my amazing boyfriend right here, and he's all I need. Thank you for your interest, though. I'm very flattered. Come on, honey. We have more shopping to do." Celeste tugged me away as the couple stared open mouthed at them. I was just as shocked but for a different reason. I knew it had been an act, but they'd called me their boyfriend. And I'd *loved* it.

Once we turned the corner, I met Celeste's eyes, and then we both broke into laughter. The look on their faces had been hilarious.

"Do you get that a lot?" I asked once I'd calmed down. Now that I'd gotten over how well Celeste had handled them, I couldn't believe how rude those two had been.

"Not really. I don't spend time around humans much, and supes don't seem to be as curious about these things. I mean, fae are known to not stick to gender norms, so I'm nothing out of the ordinary to them."

"That makes sense. Well, if another human ever annoys you like that, feel free to bring them to the shop. I know of a poison that has just the right amount of magic to be untraceable by any human test and causes some wicked stomach problems," I said with a wink, and Celeste smiled widely, which was what I'd been aiming for.

"I'll keep that in mind. Now, shall we actually get started with the shopping?"

Honestly, just walking around TOSS with Celeste felt perfect, but I knew we needed to get the shopping done, so I nodded in agreement.

Celeste didn't drop my hand as they started walking, and I couldn't keep a smile from stretching my lips.

SIX

Celeste

"Oh, that's a pretty scarf. Were you thinking of getting it for Iris?" I asked as I walked closer to Hector.

He shook his head as he rubbed his thumb against the woolen scarf. I copied his move, surprised at how soft it was. I just might get one for myself. "Iris's mom, actually. She loves scarves." He lifted the small tag hanging from it and raised a brow. "Oh, someone local made it. Noel Snow, it says."

I smiled at the name, and Hector raised a brow at me. "You know them?"

I shrugged. "Kind of. I know *of* him. He's an elf I believe. Lives in the Christmas tree farm on the other side of town with the shifter pack. Oh, we should go there! Get a tree for our places!"

Hector stared at me for so long I wondered if I'd messed up somehow. Maybe I was rushing again. Damn it. "Sorry, never mind. I'm getting ahead of myself."

He shook his head then, his free hand covering mine. "Oh no, not at all. I'd love to do that with you."

I smiled widely at that, relief washing through me. How was it I'd managed to pair up so many supes and help them find their happiness, and yet I was so bad at this dating thing myself?

"Awesome! And you should definitely get that for Iris's mom. I think she'll love it."

"Yeah, I think so too. Did you find anything yet?"

"Not really. My brother would wear board shorts and tank tops every day if he could, so I don't think I'll find anything for him here," I admitted with a roll of my eyes. Tharion was an excellent king and an awesome brother, but his fashion sense was awful.

Hector chuckled. "Does he live around here?"

I shook my head, biting my lip. I needed to tell Hector everything, and soon, but I couldn't do it in public. The last thing I needed was for a supe to find out about the other realms.

There was a time when I'd lived among the humans as my true self, but I'd quickly realized I couldn't help everyone. People got reckless when they realized even Fate couldn't help them, and recklessness usually led to hate, which led them to try to harm me. They never managed to, but they did end up earning a one-way ticket to the Burning Chasm.

"No, not here. There are things I need to tell you, Hector, but not here. Maybe we could have dinner at my place? Just as friends if that's what you'd prefer, but I'd like to have everything out in the open early on."

Hector watched me for a moment, head tilted as he thought over my words. "Is it something... bad?"

I shook my head. "Not really. I just want you to know everything about me, and I can't tell you most of it public."

Hector nodded slowly before the barest of smiles curved his lips. "On one condition," he decided.

"Anything."

"I don't want it to be a just-friends dinner," he said, and I grinned as butterflies took flight in my belly.

"Deal. Though I have to confess the food will be ordered in. I can't cook. At all," I admitted. Since I lived in a realm where I could have a feast on my table with just a thought, I had long forgotten the art of cooking.

"Good to know," Hector said with a chuckle. "I'm not the best at cooking either. Tea is my specialty."

"I could live on your tea alone," I said, not even meaning it as a joke. I didn't need food to survive, so I could very well do it if he let me.

"Don't flatter me," Hector said with a roll of his eyes, and I grinned at him.

****

After a few hours of shopping, we headed back to the tea shop, and Iris waved at us the moment we stepped inside.

"Hey, you two! Good shopping?" I nodded with a grin, and Iris smirked. "Looks like you had fun."

"We did," Hector admitted, and my heart warmed at his admission. "Would you like some tea, Celeste?"

"Can I watch? You said I could watch," I asked eagerly as I walked closer to him, and Iris laughed.

"Uh, if you want," Hector said hesitantly, and I smiled again.

"I do, very much."

Hector shook his head as if he couldn't comprehend why I'd want to but let me follow him into the kitchen. I closed the door and leaned against it so I wouldn't be in the way, watching him as he washed his hands thoroughly before installing himself at his station.

He was quiet as he worked, and I didn't mind one bit. Instead, I took the opportunity to take all of him in, taking my time with each unique feature. His dark brown eyes were the color of black tea, deep and soulful. His short black hair fell against his forehead, just long enough to run my fingers through it. He bit his lower lip as he added something to the tea, and my eyes shifted to it, wishing I could be the one biting it. Patience, Celeste.

He pushed his sleeves up as he worked, and that's when I saw it. His right forearm was covered in tattoos. Beautiful vines were wrapped around his arm, bright purple flowers blooming against his skin. I'd never seen anything so beautiful before. He was mesmerizing, his every feature making me even more curious about him. Like the piercings down the sides of his ears that I'd somehow missed earlier. Were they part of a rebel phase, or did he just get them because he liked them? What about the tattoos? Did the beautiful flowers represent a cherished memory ?

I wanted to know all about this beautiful man, and hopefully, I'd have a long, long time to get to know each and every part of him.

Hector

"This is marvelous," Celeste gushed as they took another sip, and I rolled my eyes. It wasn't even one of my special teas, just a simple ginger and honey blend I'd been experimenting with.

"I'm glad you like it," I said, smiling into my cup.

"Dinner tonight?" they asked softly, and I nodded, reminding myself they were my mate and would never abandon me. I wondered what they wanted to tell me, but

I knew that if I thought about it for too long, I'd end up drowning myself in anxiety.

"I'll send you my address," Celeste said as they pulled their phone out, and I smiled at their eagerness. At least I wasn't the only one feeling all kinds of emotions over this. I'd gone from not wanting to risk my heart to throwing it at this beautiful person so quickly it had left me with whiplash, but I couldn't bring myself to regret it. Something told me the risk was worth taking, and I had to trust that instinct.

My phone pinged, and I knew it was a text from Celeste. "Perfect. Does eight work? The shop closes at seven, and I need to help Iris with clean up and stuff," I said, and they smiled.

"Sounds good." They glanced at their watch before looking back up at me. "I have to... work for a while, so I'll let you get back to work as well. See you this evening?"

I nodded, and they stepped closer as if they wanted to kiss me. I looked up at them, eyes wide, wondering if I was ready. It had been so long since I'd last kissed someone.

Smiling, they pressed a chaste kiss to my cheek before placing their teacup in the sink. They walked back to the door, smiled at me one last time, and walked out of the kitchen.

I sank back against the counter, my heart thundering in my chest. I pressed my palm to my cheek. I could still feel their lips against it, warm and soft.

I pulled my phone out and opened our chat thread, smiling at their address before tapping out a text.

Me: I had a wonderful day with you. See you later.

Five minutes later, my phone beeped with a response.

Celeste: Today was the best maybe-first-date ever. Can't wait for tonight!

I smiled at their response before putting my phone away and focusing on my work. Counting down the minutes until our dinner date would be a little desperate, wouldn't it?

Almost six hours to go.

Celeste's house was exactly how I'd imagined it. The cabin was cute and looked almost as if it had grown there like the greenery that surrounded it. Weeds grew out of the brick exterior, and moss covered the red bricks, giving the cabin an almost magical feel. Was it some side effect of Celeste's fae magic, or was that just how the cabin looked?

Shaking my head, I walked up the short steps and knocked on the door, my earlier nerves returning now that I focused on what I was there for. A date with Celeste. Where they also wanted to tell me something, something so important they couldn't share it in a public space. The question of what it could be had kept going around and around in my mind all day, and I was just about ready to have it all out in the open, but I knew I needed to be patient.

The door opened, and Celeste stepped outside, a wide smile on their face. I smiled up at them, and they pulled me into a hug, startling me. Their arms were warm around me, and after a slight hesitation, I sank into the embrace, pulling them close. It felt good, hugging someone other than Iris. No, that wasn't right. It felt good because I was hugging Celeste, my mate.

"Hey, you look beautiful," I said as I pulled back and took them in from head to toe. They were dressed in their usual outfit of a long, trailing gown, but instead of silk, this one had a lace skirt that trailed behind them, giving their gown an almost feathery look.

They smiled as they looked at me, their green eyes bright. "You look pretty stunning as well. Come on in," they said, and I followed them into the cabin, smiling as I looked around. Little trinkets and colorful decor brightened up the room, and a bead curtain separated the living room from the rest of the house. The best way to describe the room would be messily organized. Things were everywhere, but they looked like they belonged there.

"Your home is very you," I said, and Celeste raised a brow at me.

"I'm not sure if that's a compliment or not," Celeste confessed, and I laughed.

"Oh, it's definitely a compliment. I love how bright and cheerful it is." I ran my fingers over the back of the couch and the colorful throw that covered it. It was soft, and I imagined cuddling with Celeste on the couch, both of us wrapped in it to preserve the warmth.

"What are you thinking about?" Celeste asked, shifting closer to me. I shook my head, but they nudged me with their elbow, urging me to go on.

"I was just imagining cuddling up on this couch with this blanket wrapped around us," I said with a shrug, hoping Celeste wouldn't notice just how much I liked the idea of that.

"That sounds like a wonderful idea. How about we do that after dinner?" Celeste asked, and I tried not to smile at the thought. I gave a slow nod, and Celeste grinned again before grabbing my hand.

"Come on, dinner was delivered already. Let's eat before it gets cold."

After a delicious dinner, Celeste showed me around their home. Their office was probably my favorite place in the house, simply because of the view of their backyard it provided. Celeste assured me the greenery in their backyard was real and not some figment of their fae magic. Once they'd shown me all the rooms, we ended up back in the living room, sitting beside each other on the couch with way too much space between us. Celeste turned to me, the smile that had been on their face throughout the night gone. "There's something I need to tell you, Hector." There it was, the moment I'd been thinking about all day. I nodded to show them I was listening, while my brain tried to tell me that Celeste was about to say they'd made a mistake, and I wasn't actually their mate.

"Well, the thing is... I'm not really fae. Well, I was, but in my previous life. Now... Now I'm better known as... Fate." Celeste watched me, waiting for my reaction. Previous life? Fate? What the hell were they talking about?

"I'm not sure I understand," I confessed.

Celeste smiled softly and nodded. "I can imagine that. Well, let me start from the beginning."

SEVEN

Celeste

"There are three major realms in this universe," I started, and Hector's brows raised. I imagined this wasn't what he'd been expecting me to say, but in order to explain myself, there were other things I needed him to understand first.

"There are a few smaller pocket realms, but only three major ones: the human realm, Otherworld, and Afterworld."

Hector tilted his head, his expression thoughtful. "Afterworld? Is that like heaven?"

I nodded. "The human interpretation of Afterworld is heaven, yes. This is, of course, the human realm. When a sentient being dies in this realm, the soul collectors carry their souls off to their realm, Otherworld, and then those souls are sent to either the Burning Chasm if they deserve punishment, or Afterworld. Some choose to stay in Otherworld, especially if they have yet to find their fated mate."

"You said... you said you are Fate. Is that true?" Hector asked hesitantly. He seemed to believe everything I'd told him so far, which was a relief. I could've taken him to Afterworld and shown him everything, but I didn't want anyone in my other life to know yet that I'd found my mate. I knew they would descend on him the moment they found out, and selfishly, I wanted to keep him to myself for now.

"It's complicated. Fate isn't a person, it's a... a power, you could say. It's a ball of magical energy, and right now, it lives within me. If I stopped using it, stopped doing what it wanted me to, it'd choose another host for itself."

Hector nodded for a long moment before asking. "And the other realms? What do they have to do with this?"

"My brother, Tharion, is the king of Afterworld. It was where I lived before I moved here, and I often have to return if I'm needed," I explained, and Hector blinked at me, the expression on his face practically unreadable.

"So you actually live in Afterworld? You'll be leaving Mistvale?" he asked softly, and my eyes widened when I realized what he was thinking.

"Oh no, not at all. I might visit if I'm needed, but I plan on staying in Mistvale for as long as you're here. I have absolutely no intention of staying away from you." That brought a small smile to Hector's lips, and I sighed in relief. Nothing was more important to me than Hector now, and his happiness was my number one priority. If he never wanted to leave Mistvale, I'd gladly forfeit my power and let it pick someone else to be Fate so I could spend my life with Hector. "Though I would like to take you to visit Afterworld at least once. I'd like you to meet my brother. And if... if you want, he could grant you immortality and make you a member of Afterworld so you can visit me if I'm there." Tharion was the only one who could grant someone from the human realm access to the other realms without taking their humanity. If I took Hector to

Afterworld right now, he'd lose his human life and become a soul like the others, unless I got Tharion to offer him a pass.

Hector had traces of magic in him but not enough to make him immortal like it did to a lot of supes. Living souls couldn't enter Afterworld or Otherworld, and while king Damien's magic had turned his mates immortal and somehow allowed them access to the other realms without changing them, Hector would need my brother's blessing before he would be allowed into Afterworld.

"I have to admit, all of this is a little overwhelming. I never thought the human stories could be based in truths of any kind, but I trust you. I... I like you, Celeste. I want to be your mate. Different realms and all."

I smiled widely as I shifted closer to him, my eyes dropping to his pink lips. "Can I kiss you, Hector?"

His eyes brightened as his lips curved into a smile, and he whispered, "Yes."

I pressed my lips to his smiling ones, a feeling of rightness settling into my chest as our lips touched. Hector was warm and solid against me, and I placed my fingers on his cheeks, scratching through the slight stubble as he deepened the kiss. I'd been with people before, back when I was a fae living in the human realm. But once I'd taken up the mantel of being Fate, all I'd wanted was my mate. The idea of getting intimate with someone who wasn't my mate had been almost revolting. So when I said I'd had a long dry spell, I meant *long*.

I whimpered as Hector's tongue slipped between my lips and I opened for him. I gasped as he practically picked me up and placed me in his lap. My knees tightened around his hips as the beads in my braids smacked against our cheeks, startling a laugh out of Hector.

He looked up at me with a smile on his face as I pulled away. I'd never seen this side of him. He pulled me in again, and I sank into him as he kissed me, the hard planes of his body pressing against mine. This side of Hector was lustful and hungry, and I was the only one who got to see it. I had no doubt he had a sexual history, but from that moment, only I would get to see this side of him, and the thought had me kissing him harder. I could feel the hardness in his pants, and I rocked against him, making him groan.

"Fuck," he gasped as he pulled away, and I leaned back so my braids wouldn't hit him in the eye by accident. "You are absolutely gorgeous, Celeste."

I smiled at him as I ran my thumb over his wet, swollen lower lip. "And you are a phenomenal kisser."

I rocked against him once more, unable to stop myself, and we both groaned. "Fuck, I wanted to take this slow. Do right by you," Hector murmured as he raised his hips slightly, chasing the friction.

"Do you want me?" I asked as I traced the shell of his ear with my tongue, making him shudder.

"I want nothing more than to make you come right now," he answered, his words a low growl that sent a shiver up my spine.

"Then do it. I want you, Hector. I want to see you unravel for me."

Hector groaned loudly as he pulled me closer and claimed my lips in a heated kiss. His fingers slid down my chest before slipping into my pants. I moaned when he grabbed my erection, squeezing it as he pulled it out. I shifted back so he could pull his cock out of his pants as well.

The moment he wrapped his palms around both our cocks, I shuddered. His skin was warm and velvety smooth against mine. The precum leaking out of his tip was enough to slick us up as he started pumping us together, his tongue never stopping its quest in my mouth.

I tightened my arms around his neck as pleasure filled my body. I'd never experienced anything quite like this, and in that moment, I knew that all the waiting had been worth it. It had been *so* worth it.

My climax snuck up on me out of nowhere. One moment, I was moaning into Hector's mouth, and the next I was racked with shudders as my cum covered my shirt, Hector's arm the only thing holding me upright.

I felt him freeze beneath me, and more cum washed over my shirt as he groaned in pleasure.

I slumped against him as his hold on me loosened. I buried my face in the arch of his neck, breathing in the scent of herbs and Hector.

"That... was beautiful," I mumbled, and I felt more than heard Hector chuckle beneath me.

I wasn't sure if that was the moment I fell in love with him or if I'd already started falling. I'd known the day I found out he was my mate that I would love him, but that was the moment I knew for sure. I loved Hector, and from now on, he was my world.

Hector

After a few minutes, Celeste pulled back, frowning as they glanced between us. Both our shirts were covered in cum, and I chuckled at the look on their face.

"Come on, let's get cleaned up," I murmured, and after a beat, they nodded and got off my lap.

Today had been a revelation. Not just everything Celeste had told me about the different realms and but the fact that my mate was Fate. They were Fate! The person responsible for pairing up millions of people. I had so many questions for them. How did they do what they did? And if they could find everyone's perfect match, why hadn't they found their own mate earlier?

I had a lot of questions, but I wanted to take some time to process everything before popping them on Celeste.

After we'd cleaned up as best we could, Celeste offered me one of their sweaters since my shirt could use a wash. While Celeste and I were the same height, he was slimmer than me, so the jumper stretched tight across my chest, but something about wearing Celeste's clothes made me happy.

"I better get going. I need to be at the shop early tomorrow," I said, and Celeste smiled as they led the way to the door.

"Today was marvelous. Can we do this again soon? "

I smiled at the clear eagerness in their voice, glad I wasn't the only one who wanted more. "I'd love to. Would you like to get some Christmas stuff with me tomorrow? I haven't decorated my place at all. We could get a small tree and put some stuff up to brighten up the place. We could do dinner after." I hadn't planned on decorating, but now I wanted to. I wanted to do all the festive things with Celeste.

"That sounds perfect. Let me know whenever you're free, and I'll be there."

I looked around my apartment, awed by how much a little decoration had brightened up the space. Or maybe it was Celeste's presence that made my apartment feel comfier than it usually did. The fairy lights and wreaths definitely made the place look better than it always had, but the best thing about this moment was the company.

"Would you like to watch a movie?" I asked as Celeste adjusted something on the small Christmas tree in the corner of my living room.

"Oh, a holiday movie? I'd love to! I've never watched one before," Celeste confessed, sounding almost shy. I noticed his pronouns had changed again, and I was once again grateful for his aura that made sure I'd never hurt him by accidentally misgendering him. He was dressed in a baby-blue sweater and red slacks, and the outfit suited him perfectly.

"I know just the one we can watch," I said, mentally thanking Iris for torturing me with holiday movies every Christmas.

"I'll make us some hot chocolate!" Celeste decided before heading off into my kitchen as if this wasn't the first time he was at my place. I shook my head with a smile as I pulled up the movies on the flat screen and scrolled through the vast holiday rom-com options, looking for something Celeste would enjoy. Finding one about a gay couple I was pretty sure I'd watched before, I smiled. Perfect.

As we'd decorated the tree, Celeste had told me all about his work as Fate. The pixies fascinated me, and I wondered if that was where the idea of cupid had emerged from. I was in awe of Celeste's work, and I had to wonder what I'd done to deserve someone so amazing as my mate.

I went around the room and turned off the overhead lights so only the fairy lights lit up the room, washing it in a golden glow.

"I have cookies and hot chocolate!" Celeste sang as he returned to the living room a few minutes later. He placed the dish of cookies and mugs on the coffee table before standing to face me. I pulled him closer and pressed my lips to his, stealing a chaste kiss. I hummed at the taste of chocolate on his lips, and he melted against me, his hands grabbing onto my waist.

"Come on, we don't want the hot chocolate to get cold," I murmured against his lips as I pulled away. He glared at me as I tugged him toward the couch, and I winked. Now that I'd accepted Celeste completely, accepted the fact he was my mate and would never abandon me, I found it easy to give my heart to him. I wasn't quite there yet, but I knew it wouldn't be long before I fell completely head over heels for him.

I sat on the couch before shifting sideways and pulling Celeste over so he was sitting between my legs. I adjusted him so his back was to my chest, his legs between mine. I wrapped my arms around him as he tucked his head under my chin.

"This is perfect," he murmured after a moment, and I hummed in agreement as I clicked play on the movie. Every day I'd spent with Celeste so far had been perfect. Was that how it would always be with him? Would every day feel like a new, fresh adventure with my mate by my side?

Only time would tell.

EIGHT

Celeste

I was just getting ready to head over to Hector's shop when a knock on the door startled me to a stop. I glanced at the calendar on my desk, wondering if I'd forgotten about an appointment, even though I was very sure I had none around this time.

"Fate? It's Damien."

Damien? What was he doing in the human realm? I glanced down at myself and adjusted my gown. My favorite thing about living in Mistvale was that I didn't have to be Fate. I could simply be Celeste and do whatever I wished to. But as Fate, I had a role to play and responsibilities. I had to act mature and look like I knew what I was doing, which wasn't always the case. While I was responsible for pairing people up, I wasn't all-knowing like most people believed.

For example, I had absolutely no idea why the king of Otherworld was standing on my doorstep. I hurried over to the door and opened it, waving Damien inside. He was in his human form, dressed in a sparkly pink cardigan and blue jeans.

"Is everything okay?" I asked, tilting my head. He looked worried.

Damien ran his fingers through his hair before giving me a sheepish smile, his hazel eyes bright. "It's nothing realm threatening, don't worry. You see, Reece is doing a big Christmas thing this year in Otherworld, mostly for Walker, but we're all excited. Anyway, he wanted me to get cookies, cakes, and all the good stuff from a bakery in this town, but I'm not quite sure where that is. He was in a hurry and didn't exactly give me directions."

"I might know what you're looking for. I'm actually headed to the same place, so I can take you," I said, and Damien relaxed, clapping his hands once.

"Perfect. Thank you so much, Fate. I know you probably have better things to do than help me with this, but I just want to give Walker the best Christmas I can."

His words proved to me that my decision to cross Walker's thread with his and his mates' was the best course I could've picked. That child deserved happiness, and I had no doubt his new fathers would give him the best life he could've had.

"It's no problem. As I said, I was on my way there as well."

"Wanting some sweet treats of your own?" he asked as I opened the front door and waited for him to go out before closing it behind me.

"Actually, it's where my mate works," I admitted, feeling giddy saying the word. I'd told my brother about Hector, of course, and he'd already granted Hector access to the realms, but it felt special every time I told someone.

Damien turned to me, his eyes wide and jaw slack. "You found your mate? I must meet them! Oh, this is perfect timing."

I waited until we were in the car before telling him more. "His name is Hector. He's an alchemist, and Tharion has already granted him access to the other realms. Oh, and he makes the best tea I've ever tasted." I had yet to tell Hector about his newfound traveling powers, but I doubted he'd be anything but happy about it.

I glanced at Damien to find him grinning at me. "What?" I asked, keeping my eyes on the road.

"Nothing. I just like this side of you. You're always so... serious, you know? I like this relaxed, happy side of you. Can we expect to see more of it now that you have your mate?"

My cheeks warmed at his words, but I couldn't deny he was right. Over the past couple of weeks, I'd handed off more and more of my work to my pixies so I could spend time with Hector. I hadn't abandoned them, but I'd stopped working all hours of the day. I had a life now, just like Mia had wanted when she'd sent me to TOSS the day I first saw Hector.

"Maybe. Being Fate is... complicated. I always felt being reserved was what Fate would do, so that was what I did." I wasn't sure why I was telling Damien this, but he'd always been a good listener. While I was close to my brother, he wasn't the best at listening to people. He was always more about the doing than about the discussing.

"Maybe it's time you figured out what Celeste would do. After all, isn't that who you really are?" Damien asked, and I smiled. Damien was strangely insightful, and I had to admit he was right. I was at my realest when I was with Hector, and I wanted to be that person all the time. For so long, I'd overcompensated for my brother's lack of structure and reservation in his life, but it was time I realized Tharion was a different person. He was a good king, and the way he did things worked for him.

"You're right. Thank you, Damien. Also, please call me Celeste when we get inside. Hector knows I'm Fate, but his co worker doesn't."

"Duly noted. Now, let's get some sweets!" I shook my head as Damien shot out of the car. I followed at a slower pace until he stopped walking once he realized he didn't know where to go.

"This way," I said as I led him into the TOSS building. The talk with Damien had helped more than he'd ever know. For some reason, I'd decided early on that being Fate equaled being serious all the time. Why I believed that when the two kings I knew were both anything but reserved in their own ways, I'd never know.

Spending time with Hector had made me see how much I missed being carefree and having fun, and it was time I stopped separating Fate and Celeste into two different people.

Hector

The bell above the door rang and even without peeking out, I knew it was Celeste. I didn't know if it was the bond we shared or if I was just that attuned to them, but I had no doubt it was them standing on the other side of the wall.

Iris was already out there, but I walked out to greet them anyway. I jerked to a halt when I found them standing with a slightly shorter, dark-haired man. A really good-looking man.

I glanced from him to Celeste, confused. The man didn't feel human, but I couldn't sense what he was either. While I didn't have any magical abilities, the alchemist blood in my veins made me more aware of the supes around me, and I could usually differentiate between them, but I couldn't figure out this man.

"Hey, Hector. This is Damien. Damien, my mate Hector," Celeste said, and I sighed in relief. I knew that name. He was the king of Otherworld. For some reason, I'd been expecting someone... bigger. Damien was shorter than me by a few inches, slim, and pretty.

Damien smiled widely before stepping closer and meeting my eyes. "Hello, Hector. It's great to meet you!" Looking at the bright smile, the warm hazel eyes, and his lithe form, it was hard to imagine this man was the king of the realm humans thought of as hell. He looked like he should be on the front page of a fashion magazine or the runway.

"Nice to meet you, Damien. This is my partner, Iris." I waved toward my best friend, who was trying very hard to look like she hadn't been eavesdropping.

Damien turned his smile to her as he greeted her with the same enthusiasm before turning back to me. "Partner? Are the three of you in a triad as well?"

"What?" I swallowed as I spoke and broke into a coughing fit. The thought of me and Iris being anything remotely close to that was horrifying.

"No! No, oh my sage, no! Hector and me? Ew. No," Iris shook her head, making her blond curls fly around wildly.

"I think he got it, Iris," I said as I caught my breath. Damien and Celeste looked amused beyond reason. "She's my business partner," I clarified.

"Now, what can I get you?" I asked, trying to get things back on track. I had no idea how to deal with the fact that the king of a whole other realm was in our shop. The only thing I could think of to do was to try to act as normal as I could.

"Damien wanted some sweets for a Christmas party, and I'd love a tea. As always, surprise me," Celeste said with a grin, and

I shook my head. Celeste loved getting unexpected tea flavors every day, and I tried my best to surprise them.

"You know what? I'd love a tea as well. Whatever you make for Celeste is fine. I'll pick the sweets after."

I nodded as I took a step back. "Why don't you two get seated and I'll bring the tea over."

"Of course," Celeste said, probably sensing I was starting to get anxious. Social situations were not my strong suit.

"Oh, hey, Hector!" Damien called as I turned around to step back into the kitchen. I glanced back at him, raising a brow.

"Make one for yourself too. You can take a few minutes to chat, right?"

I nodded before slipping into the kitchen. I gathered the utensils before mulling over what to make. Something fancy? Something new?

In the end, I went with some old-school ginger and cinnamon tea, thinking it would be apt for the season. Once I had the tea ready, I placed the pot, three cups and saucers, cream, and sugar on a serving tray before taking it out into the main area.

"Ooh, take this!" Iris said as she placed a dish with three cookies on it. I gave her a grateful smile before carrying everything to the table Celeste and Damien had claimed.

"I didn't think he'd grow that fast to be honest. Do you think it's because he's technically a soul and his body is just a representation of his soul like everyone in Otherworld? So if he grows faster than normal, learns things faster, his body will also grow at an increased speed?" Damien asked, and my brows crinkled. I didn't think I was supposed to have heard that.

"Um, I can leave if you two need to talk," I offered as I added just enough sugar to Celeste's tea before placing the cup and saucer in front of them.

"Not at all. I was talking about my son," Damien said with a smile, and I was even more puzzled than before. Not wanting to pry, I returned his smile before treating his tea the way he requested and offering it to him.

Celeste hummed as they took a sip, and I smiled as I took a seat. It didn't matter what blend I made, Celeste seemed to always love them.

"So, Hector, we're having a Christmas party in Otherworld the day before Christmas, and I was hoping you and Celeste would join us. It's my son's first Christmas with our family, and I would be honored if you'd attend," Damien said, and I blinked, stunned. A Christmas party in Otherworld? The same realm that was portrayed as hell in human lore ?

I glanced at Celeste to find them watching me, a brow raised in question. It was my call, huh?

I sucked in social settings. I had absolutely no understanding of small talk or social cues. But I was curious about Otherworld. I mean, how many almost humans got the chance to visit a different realm without dying?

I took a deep breath and blew it out slowly. Celeste would be there with me, and I knew they wouldn't let anything embarrassing happen. With Celeste, I could very well visit hell without fear.

"Thank you so much for inviting us. We'd love to join you."

The smile on Celeste's face told me I'd made the right call, and I smiled back at them, feeling that familiar sense of awe. This beautiful, magnificent person was my mate. How had I ever gotten so lucky?

NINE

Celeste

"How are the plans for the app going? Any progress yet?" I asked Mia as I leaned back in my chair.

Almost four years ago, I'd used an app called Cuddle 4 Hire to bring together two humans, Artemus and Reece, who later found their third mate in Damien, the king of Otherworld. While I'd done that to put things in motion for Damien and the rest of Otherworld, the idea of using an app to bring mates together had stayed with me.

It was easier for supes to find their mates since the majority of them could sense their mates one way or another. But humans were much more complicated. They needed time to develop bonds, and they'd never know who their mate truly was unless they spent time getting to know them. That, coupled with their short lifespans, meant that unless their mate was a supe, humans rarely recognized their mates even when I made them cross paths with each other.

I wanted to change that. I wanted to give them a fighting chance to claim their happiness, which was why the idea of using an app had stuck. I was hoping to create an app similar to a dating app but that would use my magic to match people instead of algorithms. The only problem was that I had zero idea about how to get the thing going, which was why I'd asked Mia to figure out some alternative solutions.

"I had an idea actually. You could ask the Mistvale Clan for help. I mean, I would, as your representative, since they don't know you're... well, *you*. I thought I'd approach the dragon, and he could figure out who could help us."

"That... is actually a great idea. You do that, and let me know what Raiden says." I knew for a fact he would agree. He was mated to a former human as well, and I imagined his mate would appreciate the idea.

"Okay then, I'm off. Are you headed to the tea shop?" Mia asked as she fluttered her wings and hovered in mid air.

"Uh, no. Not today. Hector said he'd be busy, so I'm just going to catch up on some work," I said, and Mia raised a brow at me, unsure if I was telling the truth. She knew me better than most, so I didn't doubt she could tell I wasn't being completely honest, but she didn't prod me about it.

"If you say so. Ciao!"

I sighed as Mia flew out of the cabin, glancing down at myself. I'd woken up today feeling decidedly femme, and it had been instinct to match my outside to my inside the way I wanted it to be. Back when I'd been alive as a fae, I would put an illusion on myself so I could look in the mirror and see myself the way I wanted to. I knew a lot of non-binary and genderfluid people felt completely comfortable in their body, but I had never been one of them, as much as I'd tried to be.

When I'd died and my soul had been taken to Afterworld, it hadn't taken me long to realize I could change the way I looked instead of just creating an illusion. At first, I'd felt like I was cheating. What gave me the right to do this when so many people only wished they could? I'd dealt with dysphoria for a long time in the human realm, and even now there were days I felt like I was faking it when I took on this particular form, but it also made me feel truer to myself in some way.

I'd told Hector about being able to represent my gender through my body, about what being genderfluid meant to me, and while I knew he understood, I still felt apprehensive about letting him see me in this form. Our relationship was still in its budding stages, and I didn't want this to be a setback.

But what about later? What would I do when we started living together? I couldn't hide for long. Even so, I could wait until our bond was stronger before showing him this side of me, couldn't I?

I got off my chair and stretched my arms above my head. My mind felt too cluttered to work, so I walked into my backyard, smiling at the bees buzzing around and the sweet scent in the air. My backyard was a beautiful place. My magic kept the place thriving even when I wasn't around, and I liked being in the garden now and then. It was a replica of my garden in Afterworld, or at least as much of it as I was able to replicate in this realm, and it always made me feel at home.

I took a seat on the small back porch and closed my eyes. Even though I'd met Hector just weeks ago, I already missed him after only one day without seeing him. Was he thinking about me? He'd texted a few times, and I'd told him I was busy, feeling awful for lying.

The thing was, I was afraid. I was afraid he wouldn't be able to accept this part of me, even though he'd said he would, or that he would lie to prevent hurting me and then feel miserable.

I didn't like being intimate with someone when I was in this form, but I adored being held and snuggled. It made me feel cozy and safe.

I wanted him to hold me and kiss me when I was in this form. But would he be okay with that?

For someone who was known for pairing people with their perfect match, I was starting to wonder if my magic had messed up with my own bond somehow.

Hector

It was two days before Christmas, and something was wrong.

Ever since the day I'd first seen Celeste, they'd visited the shop every single day. They would drop by, order a different tea, and then we'd go wherever we were planning to. Or if we had no plans, they'd just hang around the shop for a bit.

Which was why the fact that they hadn't visited yet struck me as odd. I'd texted them a few times, and even the replies had been... off. They'd said they were busy, but for some reason, I felt like they were lying.

Which was why I'd taken a half day and was on my way to their place. I knew very well that I could be overreacting, but my gut told me Celeste needed me, and if foster homes had taught me anything, it was to trust my instincts.

I parked my car in her driveway before getting out and walking to the front door. I knocked before calling out, "Celeste? It's Hector."

I heard sounds of shuffling before the door opened and there she was. Dressed in a shirt I was pretty sure was mine, Celeste looked... different. Her hair was still in its usual braids and her pale green eyes were wide as she watched me as if waiting for me to say something.

"Are you okay? I know you said you were busy, but something felt... off." Without waiting for a reply, I pulled her into a hug, wrapping my arms tightly around her waist. And that was when it clicked.

I hadn't even realized I had used she/her pronouns for her since the moment I arrived, but holding her in my arms, it was pretty clear. Where I was used to feeling hard planes, all I felt were curves. Celeste had told me about her magic before, but I'd almost forgotten about it. She'd told me there were days when she felt more comfortable in a female body, when she wanted to be seen as a woman. She'd sounded worried even when she'd told me, and I'd assured her I wanted her to be true to herself, but apparently I hadn't done a good enough job if that was why she'd stayed home today.

"Hector, I..." she whispered, and her voice was the same as always, because no matter what, Celeste would always be Celeste.

"Shh... Was this what you were worried about? You don't need to hide from me, Celeste."

I pulled away from her and took her hand as I led her into the cabin, closing the door behind us. I led her to the couch and settled in beside her, taking her hands in mine.

"Celeste, you mean the world to me. And I love every part of you, okay?"

Celeste's lips parted in shock, her eyes glimmering. She squeezed my hands tightly before throwing her arms around me. I laughed as I pulled her into my lap, her legs spreading out on the couch.

"I love you too," she murmured as she placed her palm on my cheek. "Thank you."

"Trust me, Celeste. Loving you is the easiest thing I've ever done." I squeezed her to me, remembering what she'd said about the kind of intimacy she preferred in this form. I didn't completely understand the nuances of her gender identity yet, or how they related to our relationship, but I planned on learning as much as I could about it because Celeste deserved that and more.

I pulled her closer and claimed her lips in a soft kiss, humming as she pressed closer to me. Her body was soft against mine, different but not bad. How could it be when my heart was full of love for her?

She pulled away after a moment, a small smile on her lips, and I played with her braids as I met her eyes. "You don't ever need to hide from me, Celeste. Okay?"

She nodded, and I pressed a kiss on her temple before covering us with the blanket lying on the couch.

"How about we watch some more movies? I know we have plans for tomorrow in Otherworld, so let's have our own Christmas eve's eve."

"Christmas eve's eve, huh? As long as I get to spend it with you, I'll celebrate any make-believe holiday," Celeste said with a chuckle, and I grinned at the smile on her face.

She'd told me she'd asked her brother—who was the king of *Afterworld*—to grant me access to the realms in a way that wouldn't kill me until I was ready to move to Afterworld to be with Celeste forever. I didn't feel any different, but she'd assured me I would be able to go to the party tomorrow without a problem, which was good because I was a little excited to see Otherworld. I was nervous about meeting Celeste's brother, but also looking forward to it.

"I love you, Hector," Celeste said with a happy sigh as I put the movie on, and I pressed a kiss to her forehead, reveling in the warmth of my mate in my arms.

"And I love you."

TEN

Celeste

For two days every year, the cliff top where Damien's villa and his small village of soul collectors sat was covered in snow. On any other day of the year, Otherworld was warm enough that most souls preferred to remain shirtless, a courtesy of the Burning Chasm that lay on the southern edge of Otherworld. The heat of the Chasm was enough to keep the souls of Otherworld warm and cozy throughout the year, something I preferred to avoid thinking about. Nothing killed the cozy vibes faster than realizing that the warmth came from the blazing fire that burned the darkest souls of the realms.

On Christmas Eve and Christmas Day, the cliff top was covered in a thick coating of snow that appeared overnight. I squeezed Hector's hand as he steadied himself. Traveling between realms could be a disconcerting experience, especially for someone who wasn't a soul collector.

"Okay?"

"Dandy," he grumbled, making me smile. He looked gorgeous, dressed in a warm brown sweater, his sleeves pulled up to show off the beautiful floral tattoos I now knew represented his love for tea. The purple flowers were called Asian pigeonwings, and they were vibrant against his arms. He looked around the place, and his lips parted as he took everything in. A wide path led straight to the villa, which was really a castle more than anything, but it was called Brume Villa, for reasons I didn't remember. A smaller path led toward the village, but since the party was at the villa, I led us that way, letting Hector soak everything in.

"Wow, this... this isn't what I was expecting," Hector whispered, and I chuckled.

"Did you want fire and brimstone? Have I disappointed you?" I teased, and Hector rolled his eyes as he shot me a smile.

"This is much better than fire and tortured souls. I'm just curious what Afterworld looks like if Otherworld is this beautiful."

I hummed as I squeezed his hand. "I'll take you home soon, and you can see for yourself. How does that sound?" I asked as we reached the villa gates. It opened the moment we drew closer, and I led Hector inside, smiling at all the colorful lights that decorated the front of the massive stone building. Wreaths hung on the villa door, and snowmen stood guard on either side, waiting to greet all the guests. The courtyard was empty at the moment, telling me the party had probably already started.

"I would love that. I'd like to meet your brother as well," Hector said, and it took me a moment to remember what I'd said.

A loud, booming laugh greeted us when we stepped inside, and I smiled as I glanced at Hector. "Looks like you won't have to visit Afterworld to meet him." While Tharion had used my bond to Hector to grant him the ability to travel between realms without losing his life, the two hadn't met yet, and I was eager to introduce my brother to the man I'd fallen in love with.

I led Hector through the fairy light-covered hallways. We ended up in one of the rarely used party rooms that was now full of souls walking around and socializing.

A massive Christmas tree stood in the corner of the room, and the decorations were top notch, making the room feel like a Christmas heaven without going overboard. Reece had outdone himself.

Damien was easy to spot in his true form since he was more than a foot taller than the tallest person there. He stood off to the side of the room, talking to my brother. "Come on. I see my brother."

"This place is magical," Hector murmured as he looked around, and I chuckled. He wasn't wrong.

Tharion looked up as we reached him, and his eyes lit up before he grinned widely, rushing over to pull me into a hug. "Congratulations!"

I hugged him back, squeezing him tightly. He would find his mate soon, but I wished it could happen now so he could feel the happiness I felt with Hector. I hated keeping his mate away from him, but it was for the best. Hopefully, he'd understand that when the time came. "Thanks, little brother."

He pulled away and stuck his tongue out at me, proving my point. He was actually two minutes older than me, but as far as our personalities went, he was the more childish one.

"Hector, right?" Tharion asked, and Hector nodded, wide-eyed. I tried to see my brother through his eyes. His eyes and skin color were the same as mine, but his hair was shorter. He had golden horns on his head that sometimes reflected the light in a way that made it look like he had a halo. He was dressed in a sweater and jeans, of all things, and looked nothing like a king if you removed the horns and the white wings on his back. I guessed he still made an impressive sight for Hector, even if all I saw was my annoyingly lovable brother.

Hector smiled slightly in greeting, and Tharion threw his arms around him as well, pulling him into a hug as he introduced himself as my brother, not the king of Afterworld. That was why I loved him so much.

Unlike Damien, who was a dead soul who had grown through the soul collector ranks until he became king, Tharion and I had been picked by our magic when we were still alive. We'd been fae in our previous lives, but the magic had changed us to what it needed. It gave us perks the other souls in Otherworld and Afterworld didn't have, like being able to eat, but it also meant we'd always felt slightly separate from everyone else. We depended on each other a lot, but after Reece and Artemus—two humans who were Damien's mates and thus consorts of Otherworld—had joined Otherworld, we'd realized we weren't all that different from the souls we lived with.

"Is that a snake wrapped around that kid's neck?" Hector asked in a horrified whisper. I hadn't even realized he'd moved back to my side, and I followed his gaze, even though I knew exactly who he was talking about.

I smiled when I spotted Walker, half-hidden behind Damien, with Ro'Shassz wrapped around his neck. He hesitantly returned my smile, and I was once again glad his path had led him to these men who adored him so much. I'd only needed to nudge their threads together a little, and I was delighted with the results.

"Don't worry. That's Damien's son, Walker. The snake is Ro'Shassz, a part of Damien's soul. He keeps Walker safe."

Ro'Shassz looked up then, staring straight at Hector. "Damn right I do. And I'll kill for him too. Kill, got it?"

Hector pressed against my side, his hand to his chest. "It... it spoke!"

"I prefer he/him pronouns, and if you call me *the snake* again, I will bite," Ro'Shassz hissed, and Hector took a step back.

"Be nice, Ro," Walker said softly, and Ro'Shassz snuggled into his neck, his appetite for terrorizing unsuspecting humans sated.

"It's so fun when they freak out," I heard him mumble, and I rolled my eyes as I turned to Hector.

"You okay?"

"I... think so," Hector said, and I shook my head. This was definitely a Christmas Hector would remember for the rest of his life.

Hector

I took back what I'd thought of Damien. He definitely looked like the king of Otherworld—a.k.a the devil—now, even if his outfit was... adorable.

The man was huge, seven feet at least, with dark horns sticking out of his head, midnight black wings, and a tail that his son, Walker, currently held in a tight grip. He wore a pink sweater that seemed to be covered in glitter, and I morbidly wondered where he shopped for clothes his size.

I looked around the room, taking everything in. Celeste had explained that souls didn't need to eat, which explained why there was no food or drinks. They'd also said Damien, his mates, and Walker could eat, but they were obviously not planning to rub that in people's faces. I couldn't imagine going hundreds of years without tasting tea.

A couple walked over to us, and I watched them as Celeste, Tharion, and Damien chatted about something related to the Burning Chasm. If I remembered correctly, that was where the evilest souls were dumped, stuck in an eternity of punishment for their sins.

"Damien, please tell me you're not talking about the Chasm at a Christmas party," the older of the couple said. The man looked like he was in his early forties, and while he wore a sweater like most of the people there, he still looked ready for a fashion shoot. His auburn hair was slicked back, a brow raised at Damien as he waited for his reply.

Damien grinned sheepishly at him. "Sorry."

The man turned to me then and smiled brightly. "Oh, you must be Hector! It's nice to meet you. I'm Reece, and this is Artemus." He waved toward the younger man. He had long, golden-brown hair and piercing green eyes. He smiled at me with a nod as Reece continued speaking. "We're Damien's mates, and also the only two humans in this realm."

I smiled at him as I shook his hand. It looked like everyone knew about me, and I wondered when Celeste had had the time to tell them about me. It warmed my heart that the people most important to Celeste already knew about me as if they couldn't wait to tell everyone.

A few minutes later, the others drifted off to talk to other people, and I turned to Celeste. "This place is absolutely wonderful and so are these people."

They smiled warmly as they looked around the place. "Aren't they? They're my family, and I feel proud to call them that."

"Someday, I'd like to move here if that's possible. Not here, per se. To Afterworld, I guess. Closer to all of this, I mean," I said, waving at everything around us. The happiness, the feeling of fitting in, the family. Everything. Everything felt right at that moment, and I wanted more of it. A lot more.

"Mistletoe! Time to kiss!" someone said close by, and I startled as I turned to look at the man grinning at us. The white streak in his brown hair caught my eye as did the wide smile on his face. Where the hell had the mistletoe come from? I looked up and found some hovering above us. Was the man magically carrying it over couples and making them kiss? Before I could ask, Celeste pulled me to them, a brow raised in question.

I smiled as I closed the distance between our lips, and Celeste melted into me, their arms wrapping around my neck. They kissed me with abandon like we were the only ones there. Since we'd arrived, Celeste had been warring with themselves over the way they wanted to act and the way they thought they should act. If I'd learned anything at the party, though, it was that these people didn't expect anyone to act a certain way. Every single person there was as real as they got, and I admired the hell out of them. I hoped Celeste would realize soon that they didn't need to act a certain way to fit in with these people.

"Can we go home already?" Celeste mumbled against my lips, and I chuckled. I squeezed them once before pulling away, not wanting to give in to temptation just yet. Sometimes waiting for something good was fun, and I knew for a fact whatever happened tonight would be much more than good.

"Not yet. You haven't introduced me to everyone yet," I said, and Celeste groaned but took my hand and tugged me along.

After a few hours of surprisingly not-so-horrible socializing, I felt like I'd talked to every single person in the realm—which was certainly possible since the total population came to around one hundred and thirty people—and I was more than ready to head home.

I had plans for my mate, and guessing from their eagerness to head home, I had a feeling Celeste knew what I had planned.

ELEVEN

Hector

I slammed the door shut before pressing Celeste against it and claiming their lips in a searing kiss. I'd waited so long for this moment, and I knew it was time. I wanted to make Celeste mine forever. I wanted them to claim me as theirs.

"Hector," they mumbled against my lips, and I took the moment to slip my tongue into their mouth, tasting the sweet flavors of vanilla and cinnamon. I pressed myself against them, groaning when my erection pushed against theirs. I pressed harder, thrusting against them as my fingers tangled with their braids.

"Bedroom?" Celeste gasped out when I pulled away for a moment, and I nodded as I grabbed their hand and pulled them into the bedroom. Their house was as cluttered as ever, and we might have knocked over a few trinkets since we kept stopping to steal not-so-chaste kisses as we traveled the short distance.

The moment we were in the bedroom, I pushed them against the bed until they fell on their back. I straddled them before pulling their shirt off with one sweep, groaning at the sight of their perfect body. Their nipples were hard, the dark brown nubs waiting for me to play with them. I focused on pulling their pants and underwear off first before quickly jerking my clothes off. When we were both naked, I kissed them again, swallowing their gasp as I flattened myself against them, my legs slotted between theirs.

I pulled away from their lips to kiss their jaw, nipping at the short stubble there. I trailed kisses down their neck as my fingers played with their nipples, and they moaned as they rose up to meet me, their dark skin was covered in a light sheen of sweat, making them look even more delicious.

"Inside me. I want you inside me," Celeste murmured, and I looked up at them. Their pale green eyes were dark with desire, just a ring of green surrounding the black. Their eyelids were heavy, their lips dark pink and swollen. They were the picture of lust, and I'd never seen anything more beautiful.

"Whatever you want, love. But just so you know, I like it both ways," I said with a wink, and Celeste smiled, a pleased look on their face as they watched me with hooded eyes.

I licked my lips and leaned closer to them, taking one of their nipples in my mouth. I tugged, making them jerk up as they moaned before licking the hard nub and giving it a soft bite. Celeste shuddered under me, telling me I'd done something very right. I bit them again, smiling when they whimpered as they rubbed their hardness against my stomach.

I switched to the other nipple as I took their cock in my hand, giving it a slow, firm jerk from root to tip. My weight on them kept them from pushing harder into me, but they still tried, a growl slipping past their lips when they couldn't get the friction they wanted.

"Lube? Condoms?" I asked as I pulled back to look at them.

"In the nightstand. Don't need a condom," Celeste gasped, and I nodded. Of course. Celeste was a soul. They couldn't catch or give me anything.

It took a moment for it to click that no condom meant I'd be coming inside Celeste, filling them with my cum. *Claiming them from the inside.*

With renewed urgency, I pulled open the nightstand drawer, jerking it so hard it ended up slipping off its track, spilling the contents on the floor. I grabbed the bottle of lube and shifted back to Celeste. Clean up could wait, I had much more important things to do.

I grabbed a pillow before placing it beneath Celeste's hips. "Next time, I'm going to rim that gorgeous ass of yours for hours, but I need you too much right now."

Celeste nodded, their eyes wide. "Be gentle. It's been... a while."

"I promise," I murmured as I pressed a kiss on their stomach. I poured some lube on my fingers before tracing one around Celeste's hole, slicking it up as much as I could before pushing a single digit inside them. I gasped at just how tight they were. It really had been a while for them, hadn't it? For some reason, the thought pleased me.

I added another finger and some more lube as I kissed their neck, their jaw, their mouth, swallowing down the gasps and whimpers that escaped their mouth.

"Now, Hector. Please. I'm ready," Celeste begged. I had three fingers inside them, and I took them at their word as I pulled out. I covered my cock with lube before lining up with their hole.

Slowly, I sank into them, watching in fascination as my cock slipped into them, the unimaginable tightness of their channel surrounding me. I didn't think I would last long, but I wanted Celeste to enjoy this moment, to remember it years later.

I kissed them softly this time, pouring all the love I felt for them into the kiss as I slowly thrust into them, groaning at just how good it felt.

I wrapped my palm around their cock, jacking it at the same slow pace, driving us both crazy as the need to climax built steadily, tingles racing up my spine.

I didn't quicken my thrusts, and Celeste seemed to enjoy the slow torture as much as I did.

My climax built higher and higher, the warm feeling at the base of my spine growing as my mind went fuzzy. I placed open-mouthed kisses on Celeste's neck as my whole being focused on that desperate need for release. Celeste froze beneath me before they shuddered, painting our chests with their cum. Their hole tightened around my cock, and that was all it took to push me over the edge.

I slowly rocked into them as I shuddered through the aftershocks, my mind a mess of hazy pleasure and love for this beautiful, beautiful person.

A warm tingle covered my back, and I blinked my eyes open to see a green glow surrounding us. I was flat against Celeste with no space between us, and the green glow seemed to surround us, rushing around us before disappearing in a way that seemed like it had been sucked back into us.

"My magic. That was my magic. It's now yours too," Celeste murmured, and I blinked again. Celeste's magic? Did they mean their fae magic or... Surely, I couldn't have the Fate magic, could I?

I shook my head, refusing to let that line of questions steal my bliss from me. We could think about that later. I pressed a kiss to Celeste's chin and then their mouth, meeting their beautiful pale green eyes that had held me captive since the day I first looked into them.

"I love you, Celeste."

"I love you too, Hector. But we really need to clean up before we fall asleep," they said with a crinkle of their nose, and I laughed.

I'd never felt happier than I did at that moment.

Celeste

I placed a mug of hot chocolate on the bedside table and perched myself on the edge of the bed. I ran my fingers through Hector's hair, smiling at the peaceful look on his face. He was such a deep sleeper, and even with his mouth slightly parted and hishair a complete mess, he looked more gorgeous than ever. Was I smitten? Yes. Did I care? Not one little bit.

I'd dreamed of this, of finding my mate, ever since I started pairing up others. The yearning had only gotten stronger when I'd encountered the Mistvale Clan and all its lovely members.

After all the waiting, after pairing up millions of people in the few centuries since I'd had Fate's magic, I'd finally found the man meant for me, and he was so worth the wait.

Hector's eyes fluttered open, and he smiled the moment he saw me. I couldn't help grinning back at him as he stretched sleepily. "Merry Christmas, love."

"Merry Christmas. I made you hot chocolate." Hector didn't drink coffee, and I hadn't wanted to try making tea. Hector made perfect tea, and I felt like I'd end up embarrassing myself if I tried making some for him, so I'd gone with the safer option.

Hector sat up, and I handed him the mug, smiling when he hummed happily after the first sip. "This is delicious. Thank you."

"My pleasure. Once you're done, I thought we could have some of the cookies Iris made and open gifts." I was excited to see what Hector had gotten me, and I also wanted to see what he'd think of my gift for him. I was hoping he'd like it.

"That sounds good. How about a shower first?"

"Together?" I asked, biting my lip as I wiggled on the bed. My bathroom wasn't too big, but it would be big enough for the two of us. I was pleasantly sore from last night, but I couldn't wait to have him inside me again.

"Mmm-hmm," Hector said around his mug, his eyes twinkling with happiness and love.

"Yes, please." I waited for him to finish his drink before dragging him into the bathroom. I used a bit of my magic to keep my hair from getting wet and turned on the shower.

Under the warm spray of water, our hands roamed over each other, touching, exploring, loving, until we were both hard and panting, our lips locked as Hector pressed me against the wall.

He wrapped his palm around both our cocks as he kissed me, and I moaned into his mouth as he jacked us hard and fast, bringing us to the edge within minutes.

I nipped at his lower lip as I felt my climax getting closer, and he jerked us harder, pushing me right into a blinding orgasm. I shuddered against him as my vision went white, and I felt my cum washing over my chest before his joined it, his hand tight around the back of my neck as he groaned loudly.

After we'd caught our breaths, we actually cleaned up and got dressed in the matching sweaters I'd bought us. I placed some of Iris's cookies on a dish, filled two mugs with more hot chocolate, and carried everything into the living room.

Placing everything on the coffee table, I grabbed Hector's hand and pulled him to the Christmas tree.

"Sit," I said as I sat down, crossing my legs under me. Hector followed suit, and I slid the two gifts I'd gotten him across the floor.

He raised a brow at me. "I thought we agreed on one gift each?"

I grinned, shrugging it off. One of them wasn't actually a gift, but I wasn't going to tell him that.

Hector shook his head before grabbing the fun gift. He unwrapped it carefully, and if I wasn't so in love with the man, I'd have been annoyed at how long he was taking to open it.

I grinned at the look on his face as he stared at the book I'd bought him. *Brewing Tea for Dummies*, the cover said.

"Oh, love. Looks like you bought this for yourself," he said, offering the book back to me with a wicked grin on his face.

"Why would I want to learn how to make tea when I can just order you to make me some whenever I want?" I teased right back as I took the book. Maybe I would read it just for the heck of it. "Okay, now open your actual gift."

I bit my lip as he unwrapped the box. I'd put a lot of thought into the gift, and I was almost one hundred percent sure he'd like it.

"Oh my god, Celeste. These are wonderful," Hector said, and I blew out a sigh of relief. He ran his fingers through the various packages of herbs and spices, pulling some out and shaking his head before putting them back. "These spices are so rare. I have to save up for months to get even one of them. How did you buy so many?"

"Things are always cheaper at the source," I explained. With my ability to travel anywhere in the world, it wasn't difficult to find the spices.

Hector shook his head in awe and spent a few more minutes riffling through the package. I was content to watch him do it. I was glad he liked the gift and even happier at the look of utter joy on his face.

Finally, he put the box to the side and handed me my gift. I unwrapped it eagerly, excited to see what he'd gotten me.

"After your gift, mine feels like... less. I should've gotten you something better," Hector mumbled just as I opened the box. I gasped at the contents before looking at him with wide eyes.

"Are you kidding me? These are gorgeous!"

The box was full of the kind of beads I put in my braids — every color imaginable with patterns and designs on the tiny surfaces and some glittering like diamonds. They were all beautiful.

"Hector... I love them," I told him, looking him straight in the eyes so he'd know I meant it.

He smiled that soft smile of his, his eyes twinkling merrily. "I love you."

I grinned as I put the box to the side and crawled over to him, throwing my arms around him. "And I love you."

EPILOGUE

FIVE YEARS LATER

Hector

After all these years of working at the shop and watching it grow, I was giving it up. Surprisingly, I wasn't sad about it at all. I would miss working with Iris, but the shop wasn't my home anymore. Celeste was my home, and I was ready to move to Afterworld with them.

For the last four years, I'd lived in their cabin and worked at the shop. Celeste had divided their time between Afterworld and me. While they could do most of their work from the human realm, they also had duties in Afterworld that they were frequently needed for. We'd made it work, but every time they were gone, it had hurt like someone had ripped away a part of me. After we'd completed our bond, I'd received some of their fae magic, and a part of me was grateful I didn't have to shoulder the Fate magic. I was much happier taking care of Celeste's beautiful backyard with their magic.

When Iris found her mate, Brittany, I'd known it was time. I hadn't wanted to leave Iris alone with the shop, but now that she had Brittany, I wasn't worried.

Brittany had been working at an infotech company when the two met, but she'd quickly taken to spending her days off helping at the shop. Once I'd realized she had a knack for brewing tea, I'd started training her, and she was finally ready to take over.

"I'll miss you, you grumpy bastard. It sucks that I can't visit, but you'll visit, right?" Iris demanded, as she squeezed the stuffing out of me with a tight hug. We'd told them I was moving to the fae realm since supes weren't allowed to know about the other realms, except in rare cases. I hated lying to her, but the only other alternative had been to disappear without a word, and I'd never do that to Iris.

"I promise," I assured her as I forced her to loosen her hold on me. Brittany smiled from behind Iris, giving me a thumbs-up. I was glad Iris had found her. Brittany was level headed and careful in a way Iris sometimes forgot to be, and I knew she'd take care of my best friend when I was gone.

The bell above the door tinkled, and we pulled apart. I smiled at Iris and waved her off, and she hurried out of the kitchen to greet the customer.

"I know I don't have to ask, but please take care of her," I said, and Brittany smiled.

"I will, Hector. Don't worry."

I nodded and took a moment to look around the room. I'd spent so many years there, perfecting blend after blend, making tea, dealing with Iris's shenanigans. I had so many memories of this place, including ones with Celeste. I hadn't admitted it to myself until now, but I'd really miss it.

"I should get going. Celeste will be waiting for me." They'd told me to take my time saying goodbye and were waiting back at the cabin for me. As much as I was glad I'd done this on my own, I wished they were there so I could hold them for a moment.

"I hope you have a great life together and that Fate always has her blessings on you," Brittany said softly, and I bit my lip. Now that I knew who Fate was, I had a hard time keeping a straight face whenever someone mentioned them, especially with the wrong pronouns like now. Unfortunately, their aura only worked when they were around. Celeste had finally accepted Fate was as much them as Celeste was, but it was still a secret only few knew. It was a good thing I was good at keeping secrets.

"Thank you." I smiled at her before stepping out of the kitchen. I gave Iris one last wave, and she blew a kiss at me, making me roll my eyes as I exited the shop.

I'd decided to walk back to the cabin because I wanted to experience Mistvale one last time, not as the touristy town it was for all the visitors but as the home it was to me. It wasn't like we had a flight to catch, and Celeste had assured me I could take my time.

Still, I didn't want to do this without them, so I pulled my phone out and shot them a text.

Me: Care for one last walk through the neighborhood? I'm at TOSS.

There was no reply, but a minute later, I heard footsteps approaching and grinned as I saw Celeste step out of an alley. Teleportation was a really cool power. They mostly used it to travel between realms, but it could be helpful in other ways, too.

Without saying a word, Celeste linked their fingers with mine, squeezing my hand as they matched my pace.

I took in the mismatched buildings, the greenery, the dark skies, and realized I'd miss this more than I'd thought I would.

Mistvale had been home for a long time, and while Celeste was now my home, this place meant the world to me too.

By the time we reached the cabin, my legs were aching a little, but the rest of me was content with the move. I'd miss this place, yes, but it would still be less painful than the way I'd felt whenever Celeste had to go back to Afterworld.

"Are you ready?" Celeste asked as they turned to me, their arms around my waist. I looked at them, taking in their pale green eyes, their dark skin that always seemed to have a hidden glow, and the colorful beads in their braids. I loved this person more than anything, more than this realm or any other.

"I've been ready for a long time, my love," I murmured as I leaned closer and pressed my lips to theirs. They hummed as they shifted closer, and the air around us warmed and tingled with magic.

We were home.

Celeste

It felt good to be back in Afterworld, especially because I had Hector with me.

I'd enjoyed spending time in the human realm. Helping the supes of the Mistvale Clan had felt fulfilling in a way nothing else ever had, and the app I'd built with their help, *Meet Your Mate*, was already bringing human mates together.

Despite all that, Afterworld was my true home, and so was Hector. Now that they were both in the same place, everything felt perfect.

I opened my eyes and smiled at the sight before me. Afterworld was a beautiful realm because, unlike the other realms, it didn't have a set form. Afterworld was whatever you wanted it to be the most, and until now, it had always been a beach resort for me since that was what Tharion wanted and my wishes usually aligned well with his.

Now that I had a mate who meant the world to me, I had no doubt this was his vision of a perfect home.

"Wait, I thought we were going to Afterworld," Hector said as he steadied himself with a hand on my arm.

"We are in Afterworld," I said, and Hector looked around in confusion.

"But that's your cabin right there. And wait, is that Aja?" He narrowed his eyes at the raven pecking at the roof of the cabin. He'd introduced me to his bird friends before, and I was surprised to see them there. Were they a replica, or had Hector wanted them so much the magic had made an exception? Either way, they were there, and Hector looked delighted, which was all that mattered. "Oh. Is this what you meant when you said Afterworld could become whatever I wanted it to?"

"Yes. Afterworld reflects the place you consider your home."

"And the cabin is my home. You are my home," Hector said softly, his eyes going from the cabin to me. I shifted closer to him and pulled him into another kiss, smiling against his warm, familiar lips.

Hector was my home, and I was his. Forever.

ALSO BY STELLA

PARANORMAL ROMANCE

Set in Mistvale

Mages of Ravenshire:
Set in the fictional town of Mistvale, Mages of Ravenshire is a series filled with magic, laughs and love. Low on angst and high on sweetness, Mages of Ravenshire will leave you with a smile on your face. Come meet Neya, Pads, April, and all the other fur-babies and their humans, vampires and mages.

Touch of Magic. (Goofy mage x nerdy human)

Sleep of Eternity. (Grumpy mage x sunshine vampire)

Angel of Death. (Sweet necromancer x snarky vampire)

Boxset. (With a special bonus scene.)

Misfits of Mistvale:
With side-characters from Mages of Ravenshire, this series features shifters, half-mermen, werewolves, and many more supernaturals. With the usual dose of fur-babies, found family, and all the Mistvale feels, this series features standalones with a different couple in each book.

Claws. (Graysexual bobcat x cat shifter)

Tails. (Merman-siren x dolphin shifter)

Bonds. (Human x femme wolf shifter x asexual werewolf)

Mistvale Spin-Off Novellas:
Featuring various side-characters from the town of Mistvale, these novellas are full of sweet, fuzzy romance, and the meddlesome cast of Mistvale.

My Elf Mate. (GFY, holiday, elf x wolf shifter.)

<u>My Dragon Mate</u>. (Bi-awakening, human x dragon.)

<u>My Elf Daddy</u>. (Daddy/little, elf x human.)

<u>My Fae Mate</u>. (Genderfluid MC, holiday, Fate x Alchemist.)

<u>Make A Wish</u>. (Djinn x Human, free read.)

Set in Otherworld

Fate's Gambit Trilogy:
Fate's Gambit is an MMM PNR trilogy featuring a sweet, subby cinnamon-bun devil, a gentle-giant who's a service sub/Daddy switch, and a slightly frustrated Master as they slowly figure our their dynamic and fall madly in love. They're joined by annoyingly awesome side-characters including a sweet hedgehog, a sassy talking snake, and a guardian in the form of a cat-man. This trilogy features the same triad and needs to be read in order.

<u>First Play</u>. (Free Prequel.)

<u>Devil's Gamble</u>.

<u>Pet's Ploy</u>.

<u>Master's Design</u>.

<u>Boxset</u>.

Lords of Otherworld:
Following the events of Fate's Gambit, Lords of Otherworld delves deeper into the workings of Otherworld, with new characters, new romance, and new adventures. With found family vibes, danger and romance, each book in this series follows a different couple, with an overarching storyline. It is recommended to read the books in order.

<u>Maximus</u>.

<u>Zane</u>.

<u>Nox</u>.

Standalones

<u>Elijah Summons A Demon</u> (A newsletter serial.)

CONTEMPORARY ROMANCE

Voice Out

<u>Weathering The Storm</u> (Roommates to lovers, hurt/comfort.)

<u>Watching The Sunrise</u> (Friends to lovers, genderfluid MC.)

About Stella

Stella Rainbow lives in a small town in India with her family and her five-year-old cat, Harry, who is her number one supporter, cuddle buddy, and writing buddy all rolled into one.

Living with a chronic illness, Stella grew up with books as her best friends, and now she writes in the hopes of giving others like her a reprieve from the real world.

Stella's books are low on the angst, high on the sweetness, with a doze of found family, and some absolutely adorable fur—and sometimes scale—babies.

You can join her mailing list to receive updates about her books and free content. You can also read more about Stella, her books, and the universe she writes in on her website, www.authorstellarainbow.com.

You can also follow her on:

Facebook: Stella Rainbow

Instagram: @authorstellarainbow
Goodreads: Stella Rainbow
BookBub: Stella Rainbow
Amazon: Stella Rainbow